LIMITED EDITION ALTERNATE COVER!

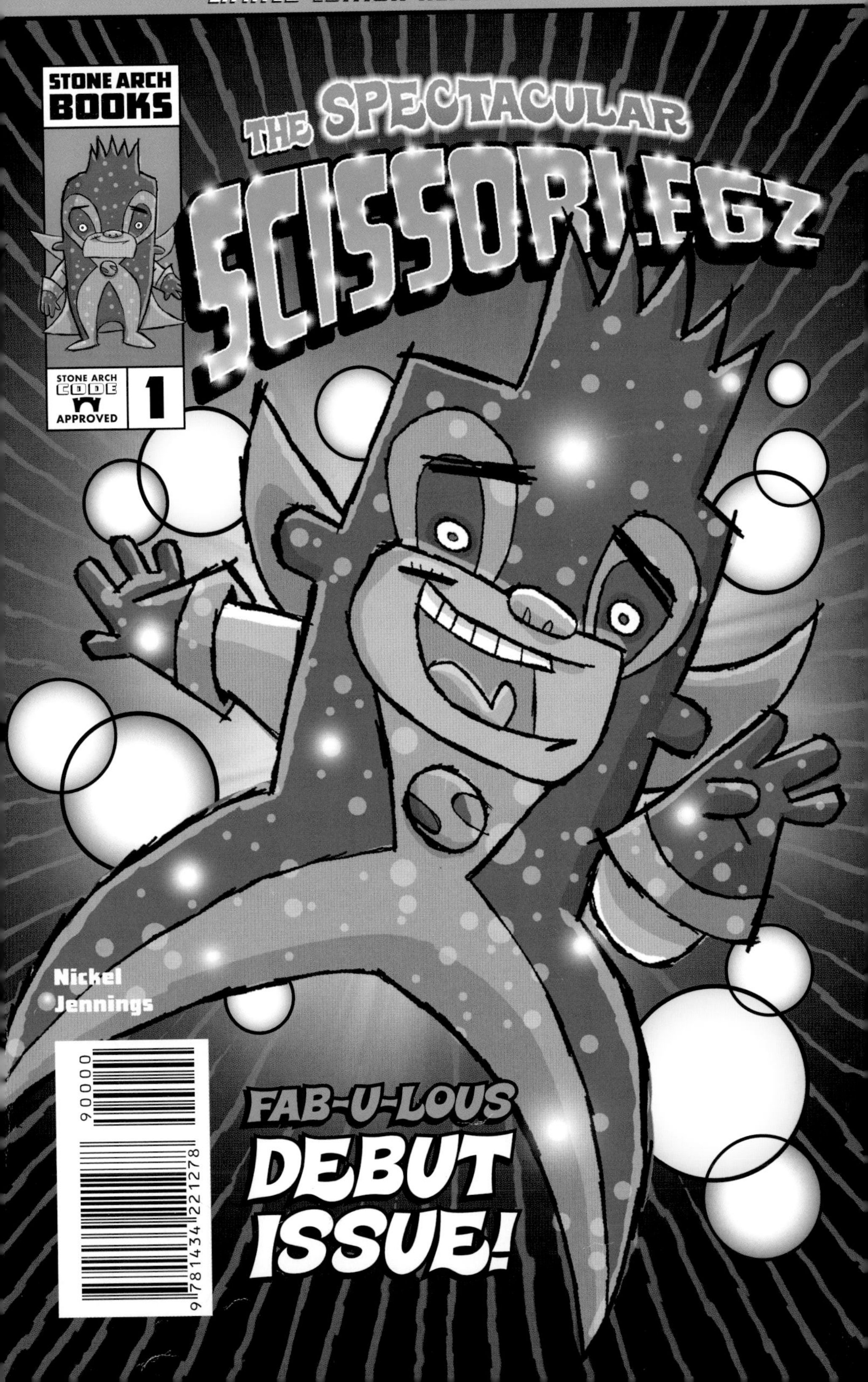
STONE ARCH BOOKS
THE SPECTACULAR
SCISSORLEGZ
STONE ARCH CODE APPROVED
1
Nickel
Jennings
FAB-U-LOUS
DEBUT ISSUE!

THE INCREDIBLE ROCKHEAD AND THE SPECTACULAR SCISSORLEGZ

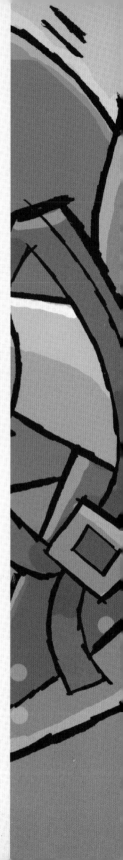

CREATED BY SCOTT NICKEL

WRITTEN BY SEAN TULIEN AND DONALD LEMKE

ILLUSTRATED BY C.S. JENNINGS

DESIGNER: BOB LENTZ

CREATIVE DIRECTOR: HEATHER KINDSETH

PRODUCTION SPECIALIST: MICHELLE BIEDSCHEID

SENIOR EDITOR: DONALD LEMKE

ASSOC. EDITOR: SEAN TULIEN

EDITORIAL DIRECTOR: MICHAEL DAHL

CASTING ASSOCIATE: STONE E. IYERS

HAIR STYLIST DEPARTMENT HEAD: ROXANNA HARDPLACE

WARDROBE SUPERVISOR: EDDIE BOULDER

STUNTS CHOREOGRAPHER: ROCKY CLIFFTON

STUNTPERSON 1: TEDDY AZIROK

KEY RIGGING GRIP: MICAH ROLLENSTONE

Graphic Sparks are published by Stone Arch Books, a Capstone Imprint, 151 Good Counsel Drive, P.O. Box 669 Mankato, Minnesota 56002 www.capstonepub.com

Cataloging-in-Publication Data is available on the Library of Congress website.

ISBN: 978-1-4342-2127-8 (library binding)

Photo credit: Shutterstock: R. Mackay Photography (cereal)

Summary: The Incredible Rockhead and the Spectacular Scissorlegz team up to tackle a task far greater than either has ever known! Their mission: to seek out and defeat the man behind countless evil experiments, the mutant-making General himself. Upon arriving at his secret headquarters, the duo finds dozens of teenage mutants — and some of them aren't happy to have visitors. Unable to tell friend from foe, the two superheroes will have to fight through the ranks of the General's minions, and make some mutant friends, to have any chance at defeating their sinister creator.

Printed in the United States of America in Stevens Point, Wisconsin.

032010 005741WZF10

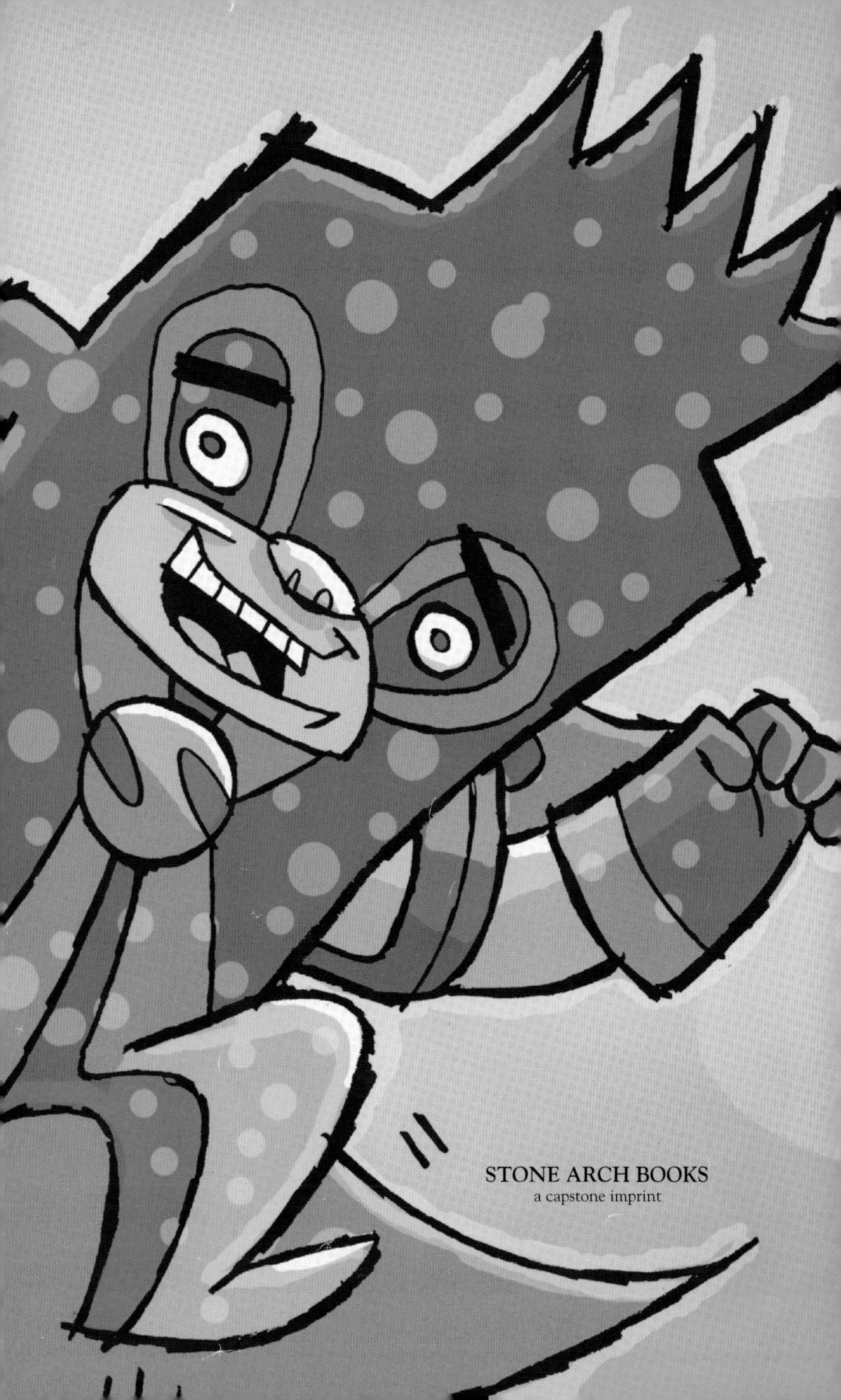

STONE ARCH BOOKS
a capstone imprint

SECRET FILES

USER NAME: THE GENERAL

PASSWORD: RCKHD ▮

ACCESS GRANTED

SUPERHERO TARGETS:

SUBJECT:
ROCKHEAD

SUBJECT:
SCISSORLEGZ

MUTANT TEST SUBJECTS:

SUBJECT:
PASTE

SUBJECT:
B. UNSEN BURNER

SUBJECT:
MONKEY JIM

SUBJECT:
MYSTERY MEAT

SUBJECT:
ERASERHEAD

SUBJECT:
RULER BOY

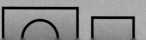

EVIL MUTANTS:

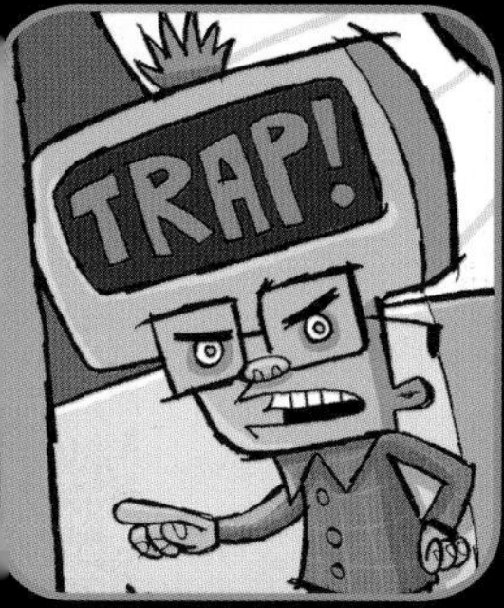
TRAP!

SUBJECT:
CALCULO

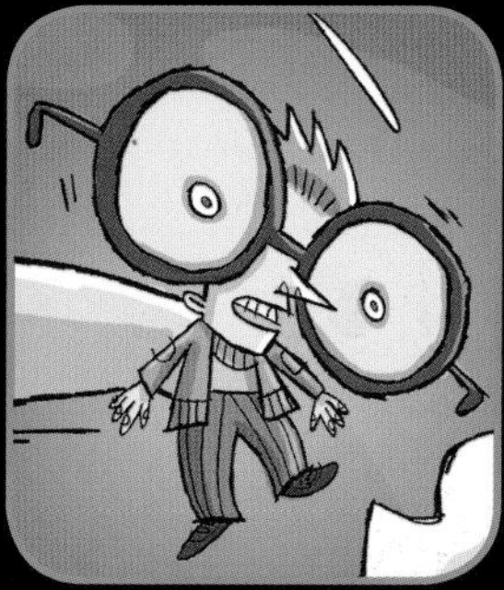

SUBJECT:
REGGIE

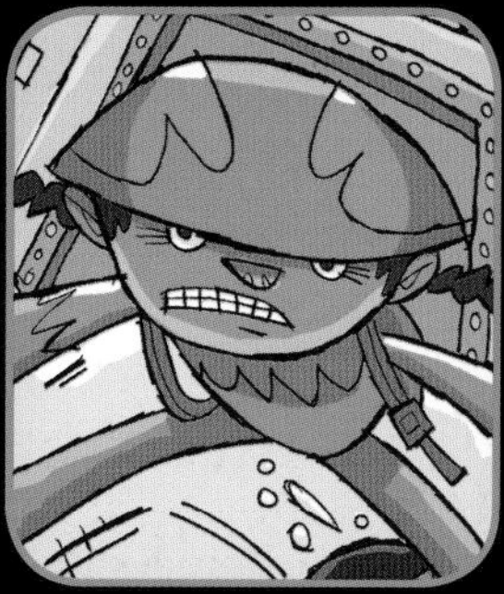

SUBJECT:
WHEELAMINA

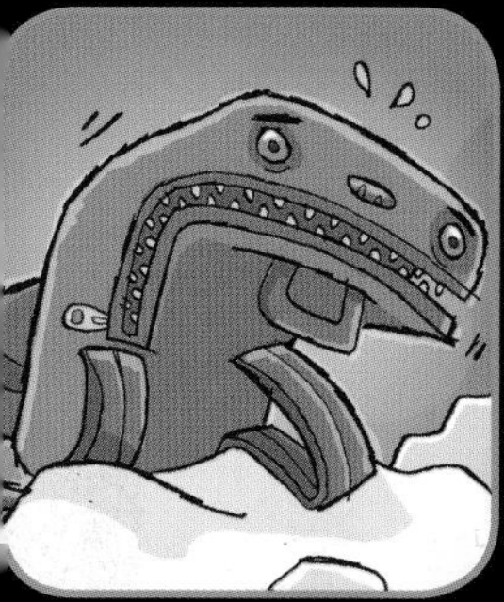

SUBJECT:
BAKPAK

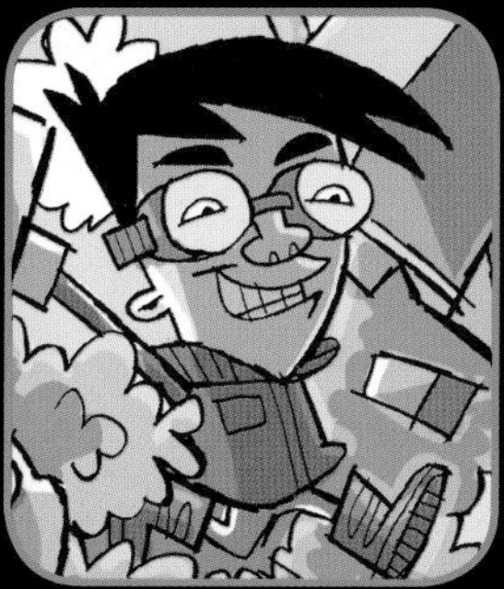

SUBJECT:
DOZER

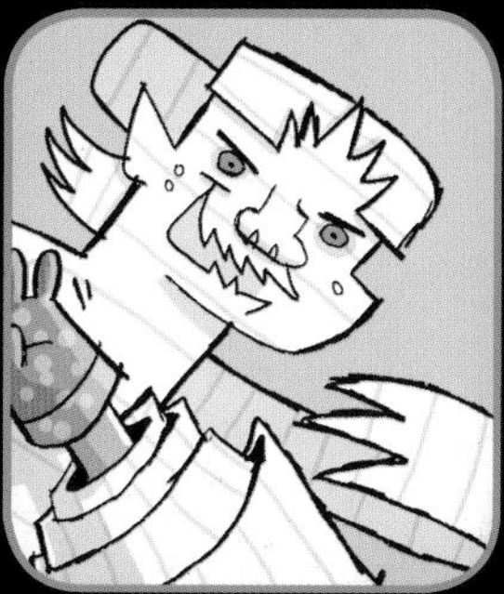

SUBJECT:
PAPERCUT

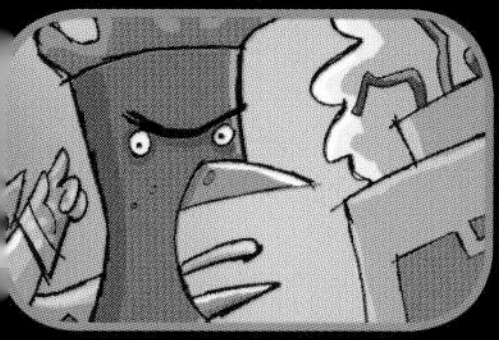

SUBJECT:
CHICKEN SKIN

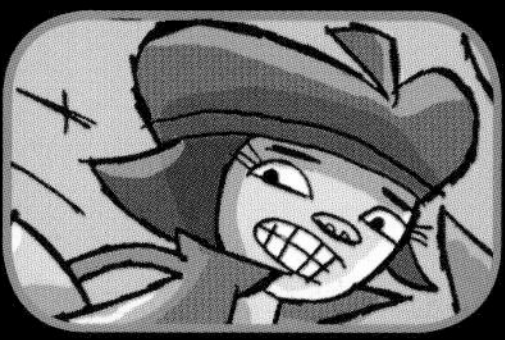

SUBJECT:
POLY MUIR

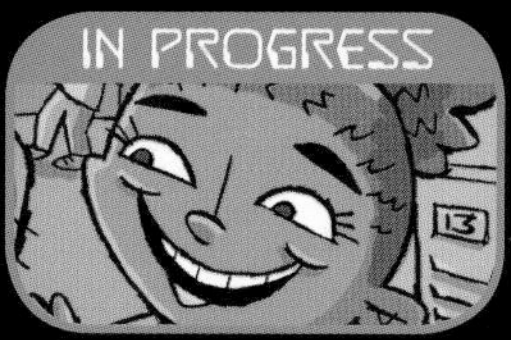
IN PROGRESS
13

SUBJECT:
JENNIFER JONES

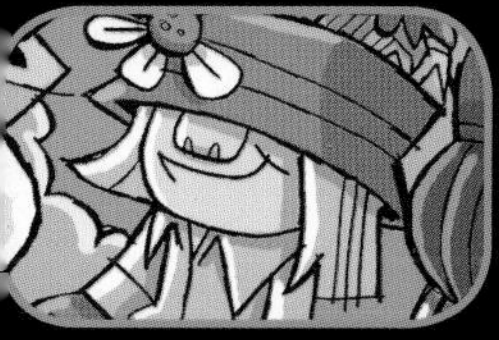

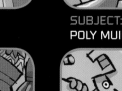

SUBJECT:
4-SQUARE

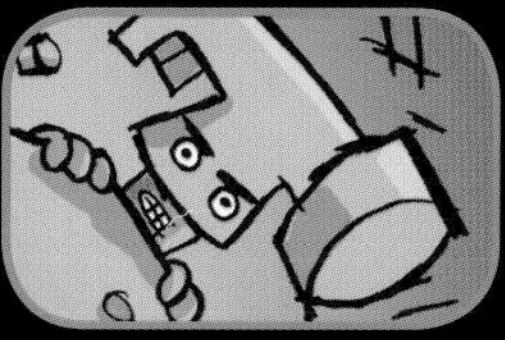

SUBJECT:
HAMMERTIME

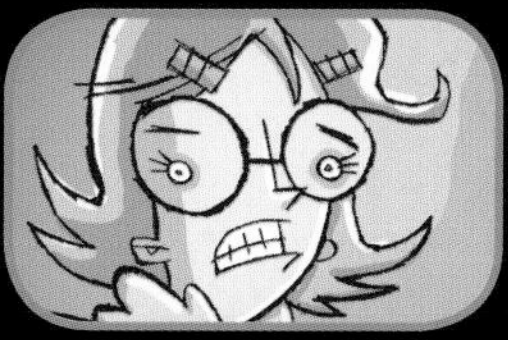

SUBJECT:
CRYSTAL FROST

STONE ARCH BOOKS PROUDLY PRESENTS: **THE INCREDIBLE ROCKHEAD**

. . . ALONG WITH THE MOST FASCINATING, MOST FASHIONABLE, MOST FAB-U-LOUS SIDEKICK OF ALL TIME:

THE SPECTACULAR SCISSORLEGZ!

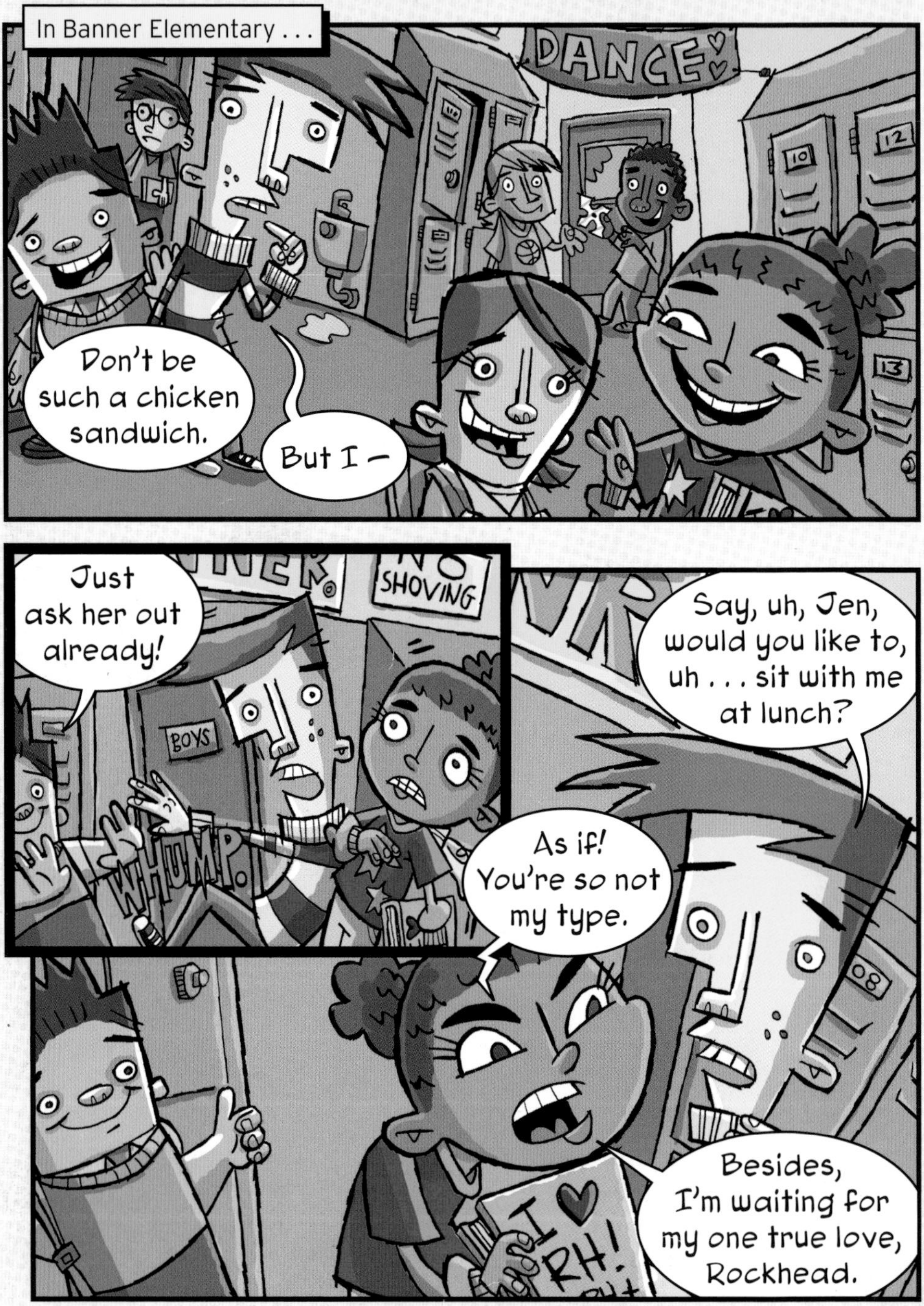
In Banner Elementary . . .
DANCE
Don't be such a chicken sandwich.
But I —
SHOVING
BOYS
Just ask her out already!
WHUMP
Say, uh, Jen, would you like to, uh . . . sit with me at lunch?
As if! You're so not my type.
Besides, I'm waiting for my one true love, Rockhead.

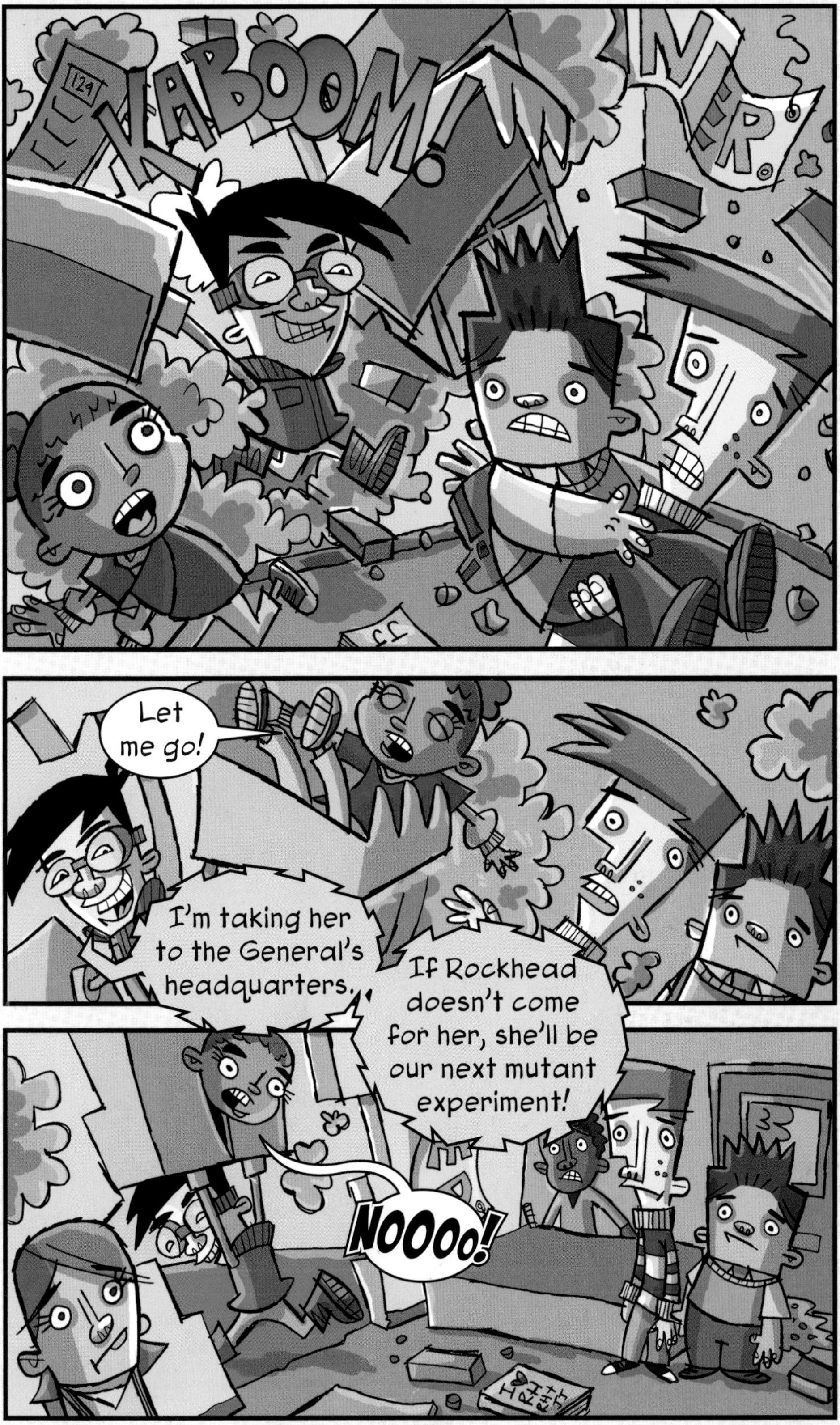
KABOOM!
Let me go!
I'm taking her to the General's headquarters.
If Rockhead doesn't come for her, she'll be our next mutant experiment!
NOOOO!

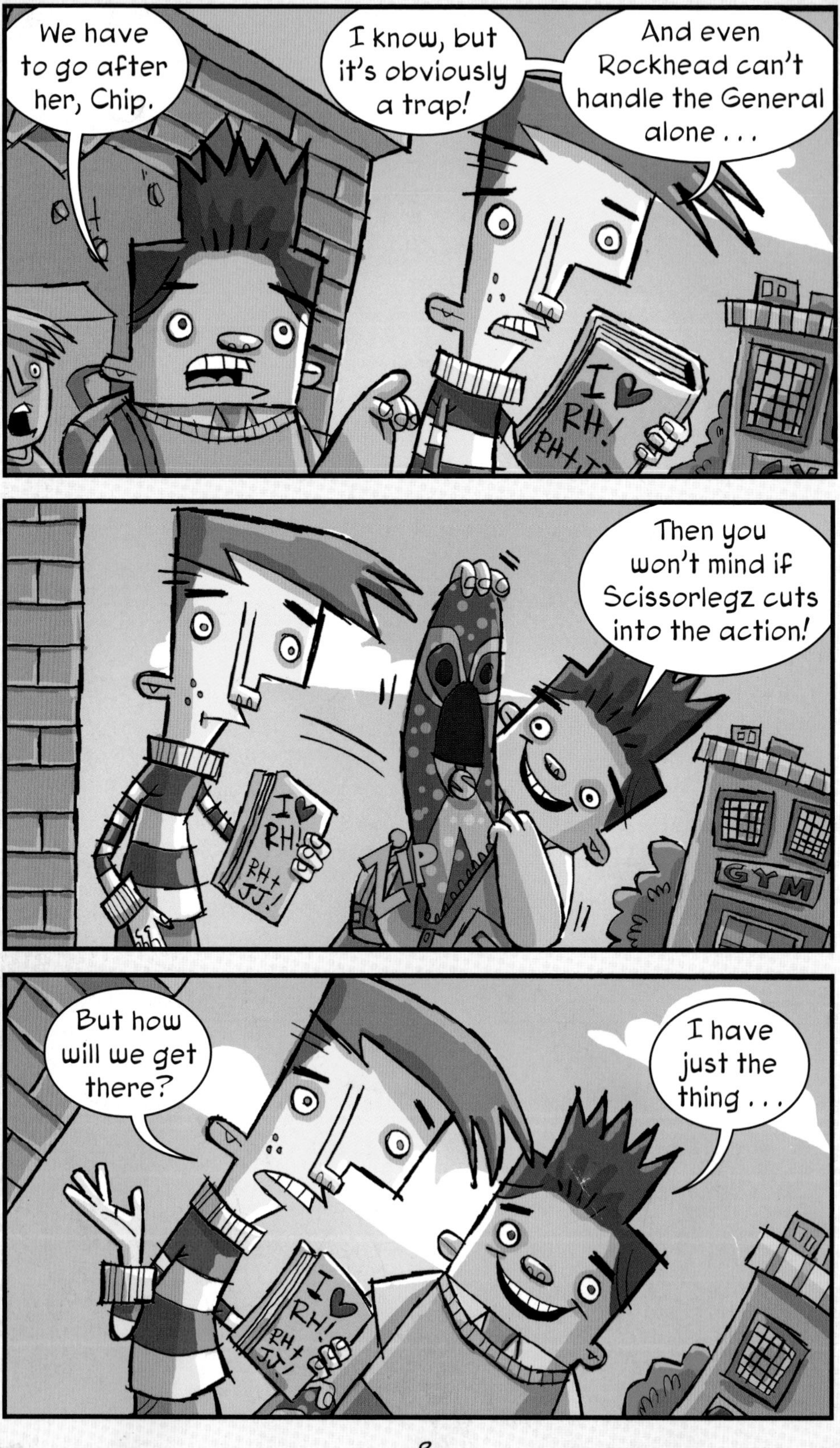
We have to go after her, Chip.
I know, but it's obviously a trap!
And even Rockhead can't handle the General alone . . .
I ♥ RH! RH+JJ
Then you won't mind if Scissorlegz cuts into the action!
I ♥ RH! RH+JJ!
ZIP
GYM
But how will we get there?
I have just the thing . . .
I ♥ RH! RH+JJ!

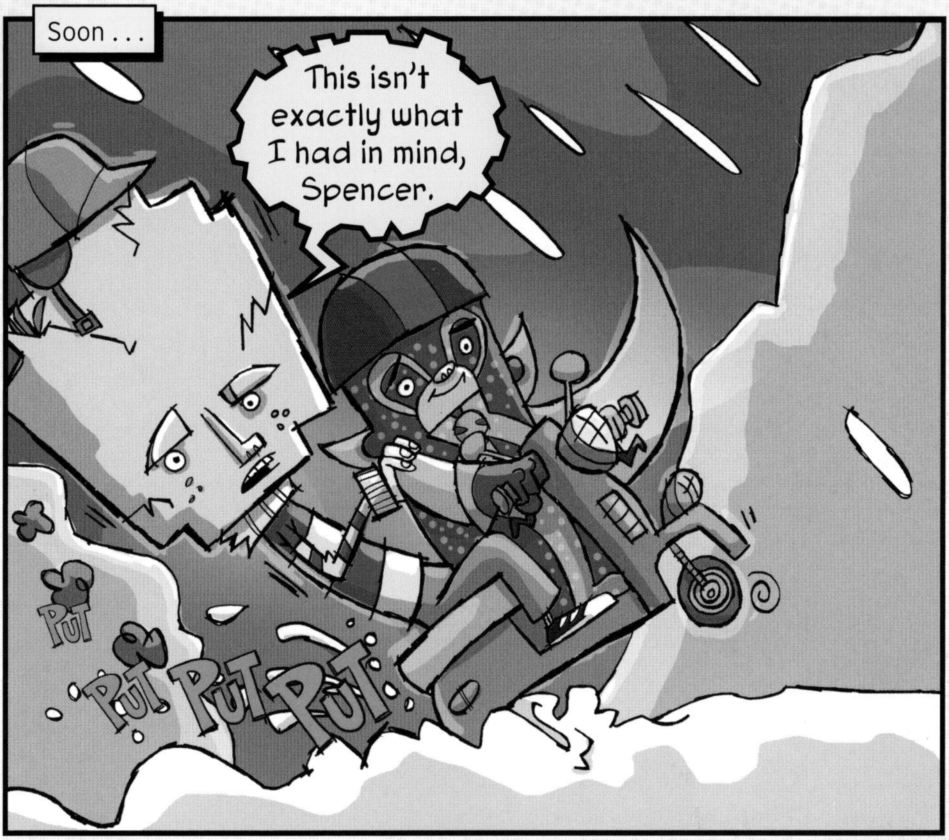
Soon . . .
This isn't exactly what I had in mind, Spencer.
PUT
PUT PUT PUT

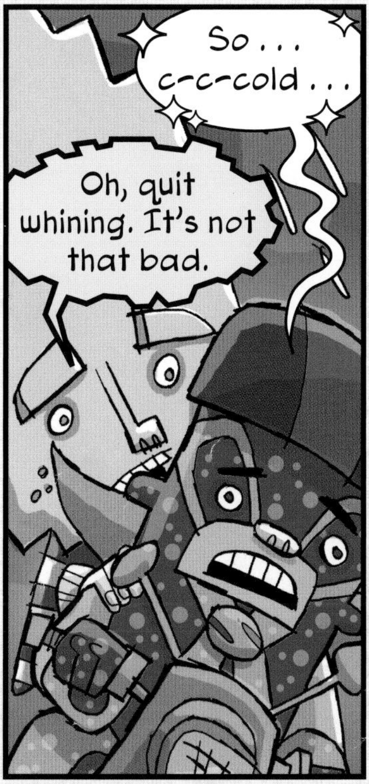
So . . . c-c-cold . . .
Oh, quit whining. It's not that bad.

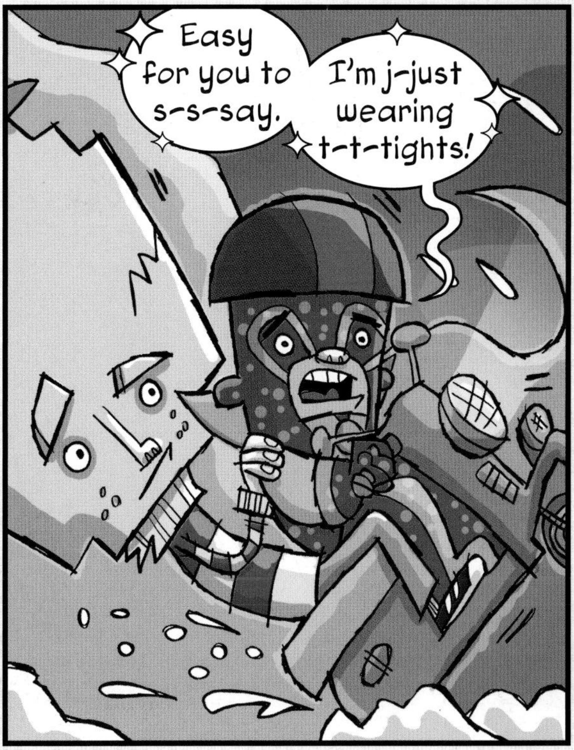
Easy for you to s-s-say.
I'm j-just wearing t-t-tights!

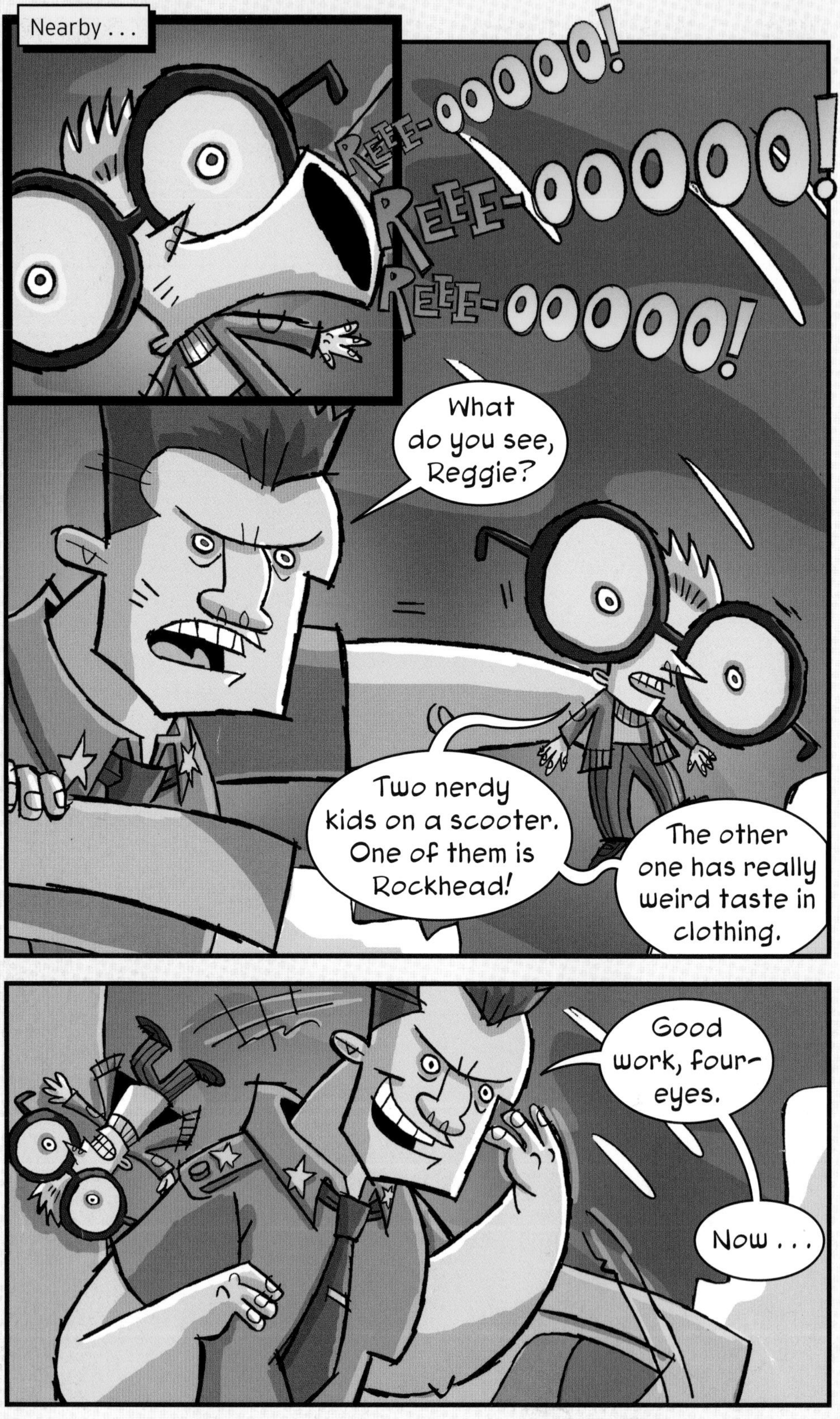
Nearby . . .
REEE-OOOOO!
REEE-OOOOO!
REEE-OOOOO!
What do you see, Reggie?
Two nerdy kids on a scooter. One of them is Rockhead!
The other one has really weird taste in clothing.
Good work, four-eyes.
Now . . .

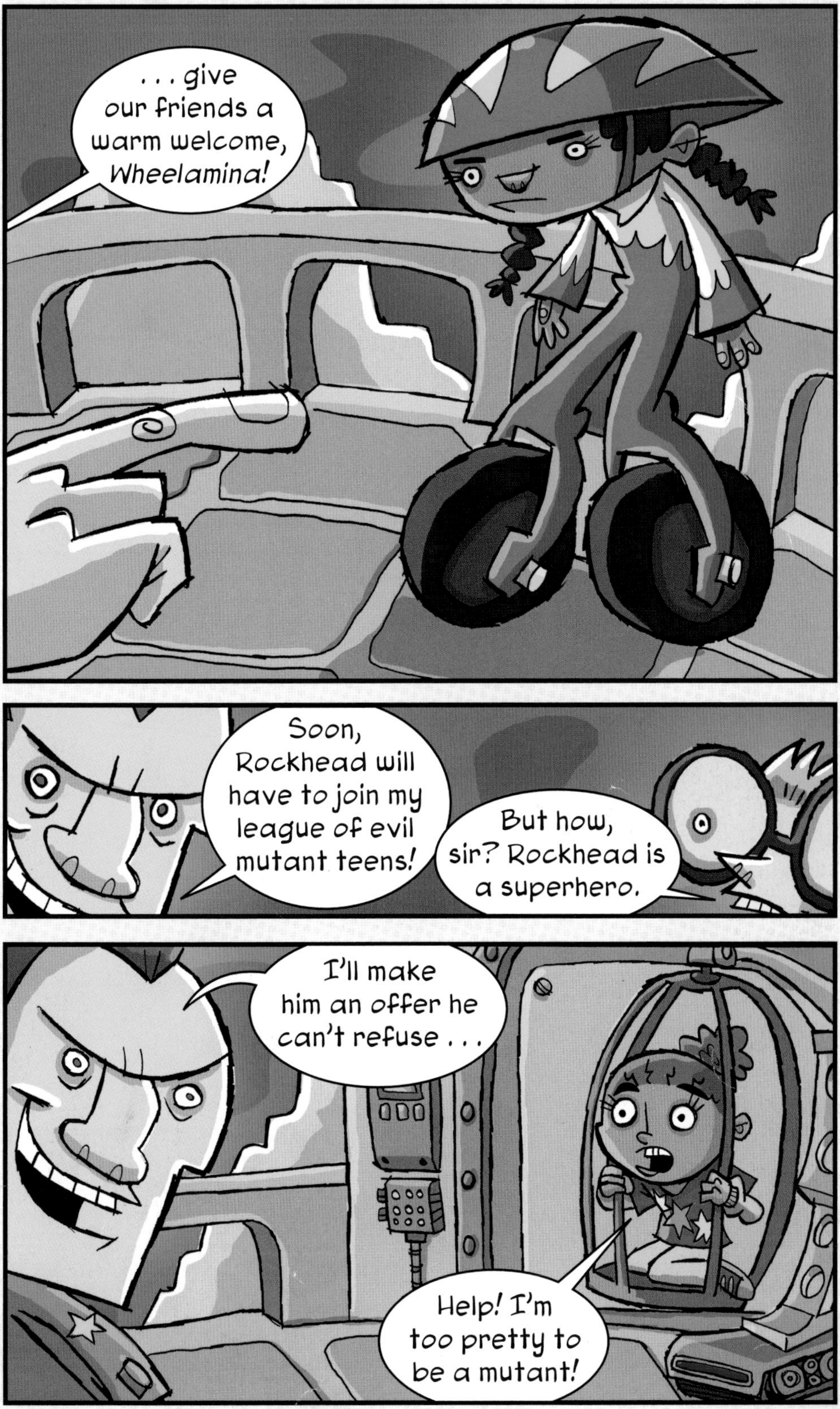
. . . give our friends a warm welcome, Wheelamina!
Soon, Rockhead will have to join my league of evil mutant teens!
But how, sir? Rockhead is a superhero.
I'll make him an offer he can't refuse . . .
Help! I'm too pretty to be a mutant!

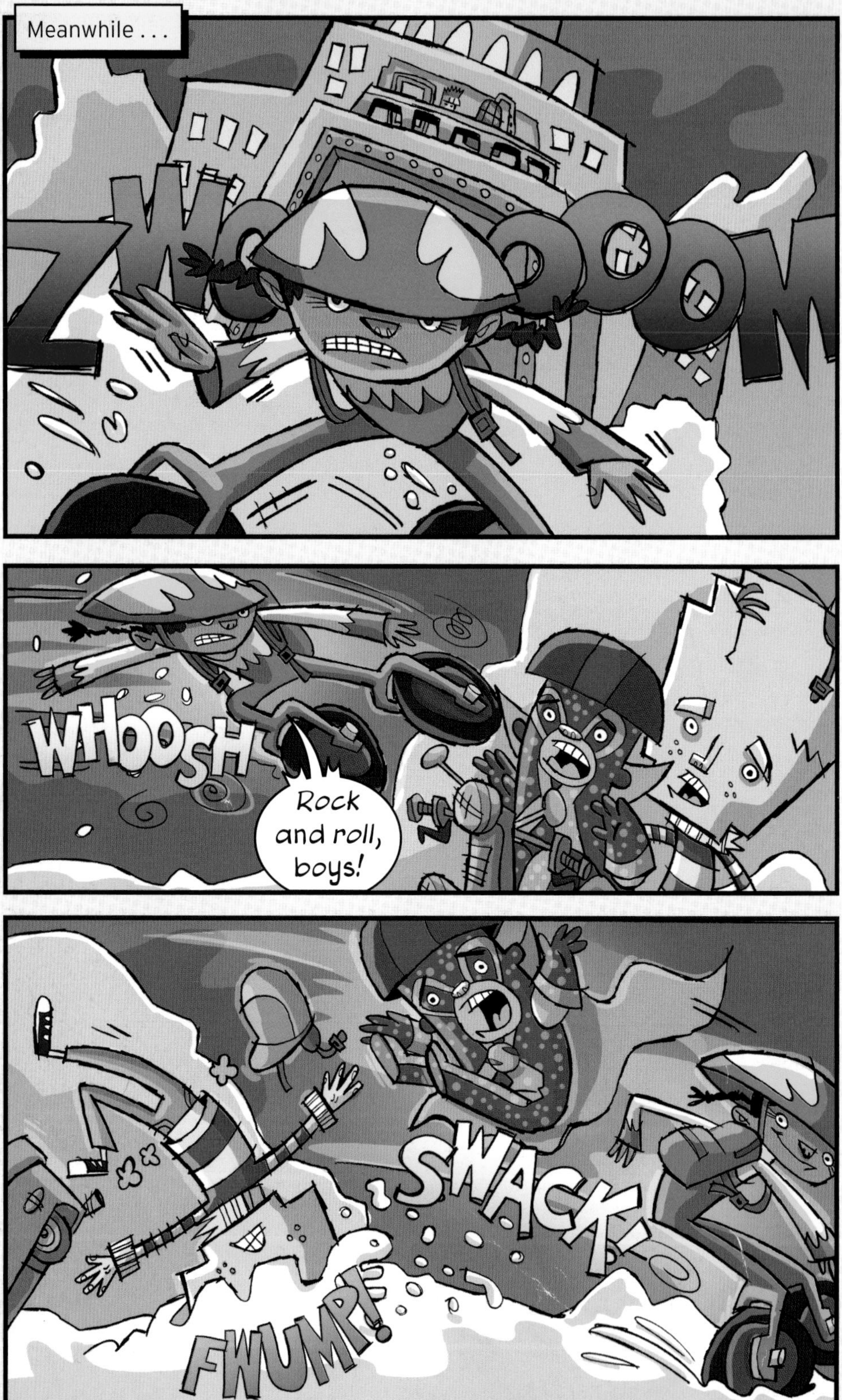
Meanwhile . . .
WHOOSH
Rock and roll, boys!
SWACK!
FWUMP!

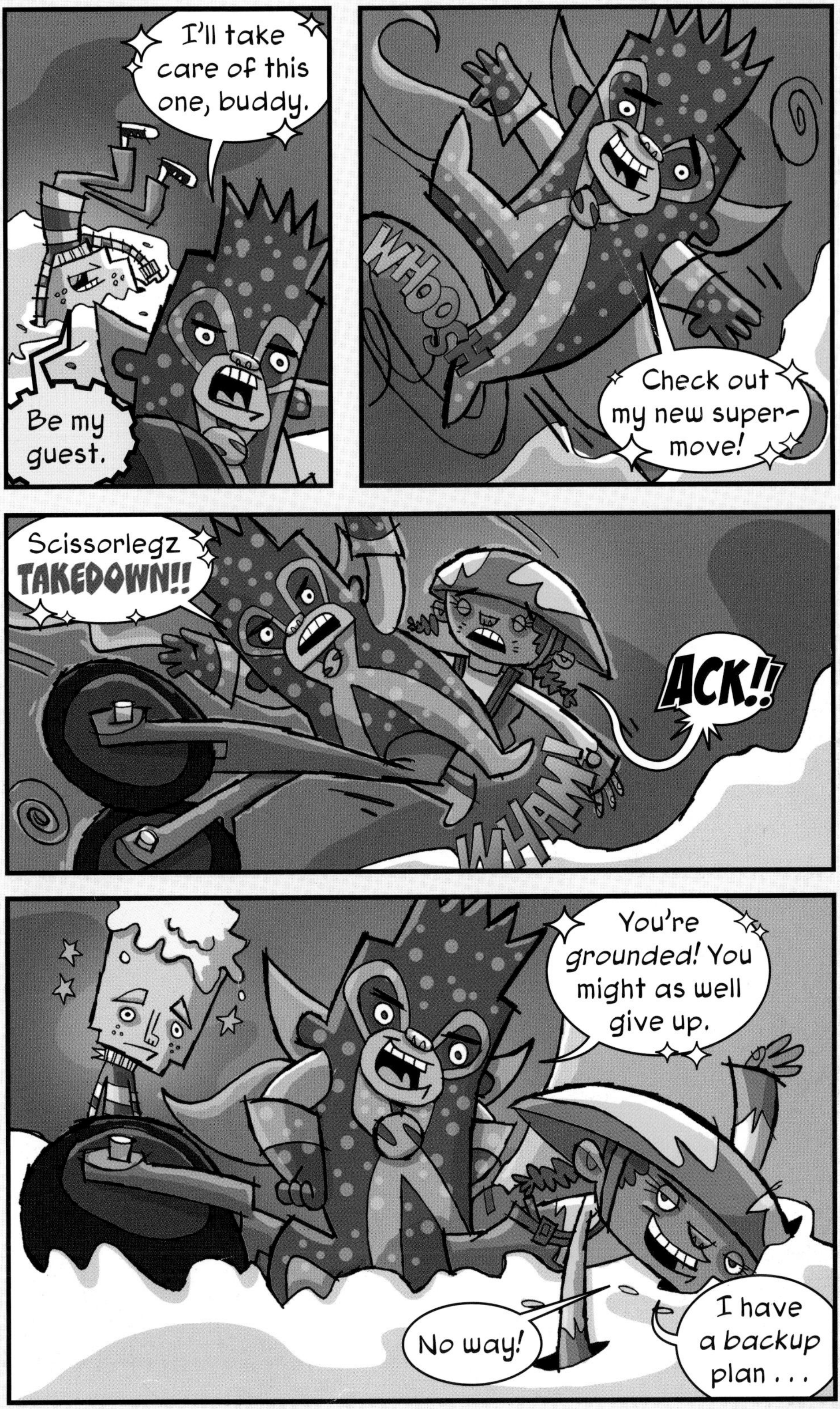
I'll take care of this one, buddy.
Be my guest.
WHOOSH
Check out my new super-move!
Scissorlegz TAKEDOWN!!
ACK!!
WHAM!
You're grounded! You might as well give up.
No way!
I have a backup plan . . .

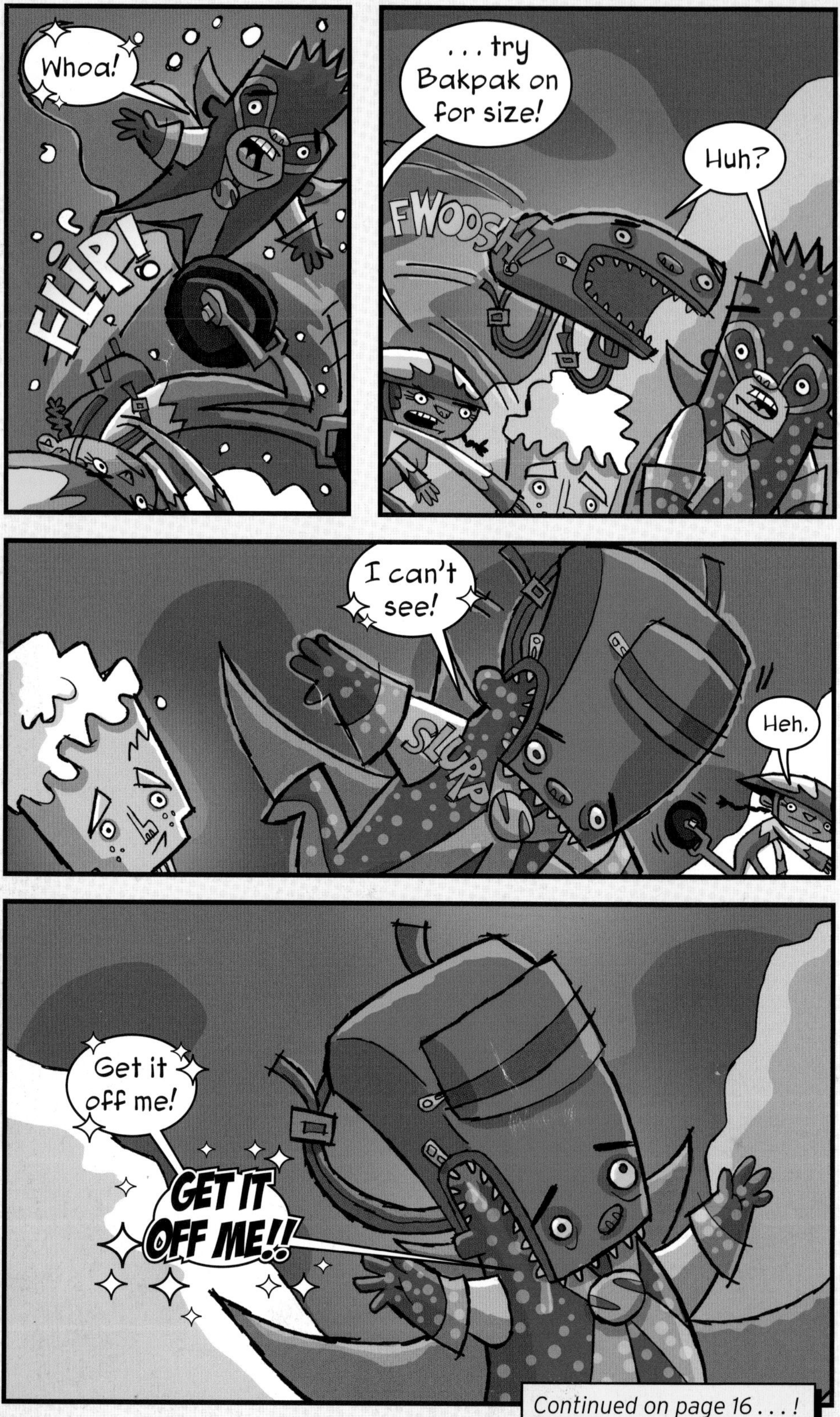
Whoa!
FLIP!
. . . try Bakpak on for size!
FWOOSH!
Huh?
I can't see!
SLURP
Heh.
Get it off me!
GET IT OFF ME!!

Continued on page 16 . . . !

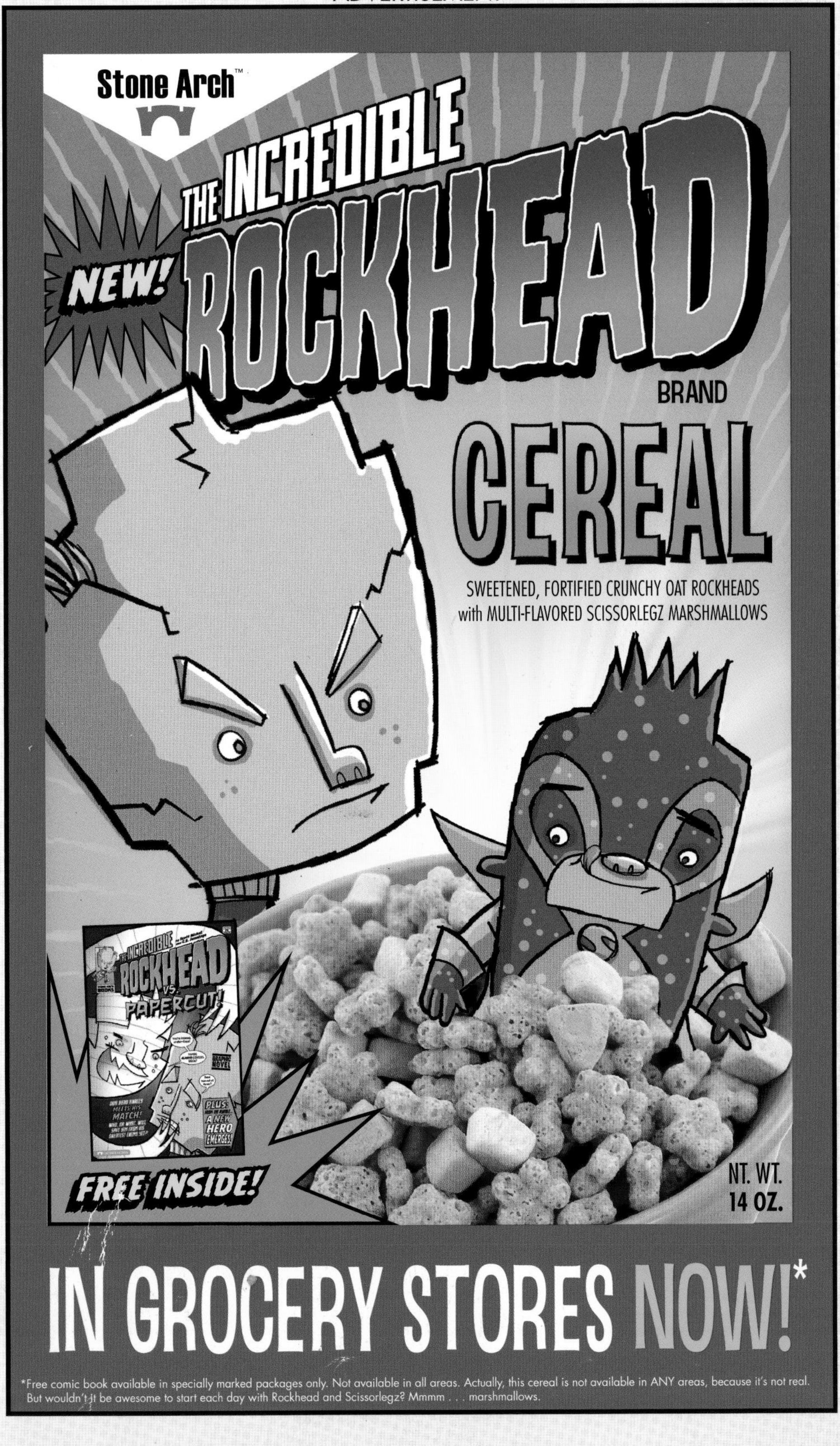
Stone Arch™
NEW!
THE INCREDIBLE ROCKHEAD
BRAND
CEREAL
SWEETENED, FORTIFIED CRUNCHY OAT ROCKHEADS
with MULTI-FLAVORED SCISSORLEGZ MARSHMALLOWS
THE INCREDIBLE ROCKHEAD VS. PAPERCUT!
GRAPHIC NOVEL
MATCH!
PLUS: A NEW HERO EMERGES!
FREE INSIDE!
NT. WT.
14 OZ.
IN GROCERY STORES NOW!*
*Free comic book available in specially marked packages only. Not available in all areas. Actually, this cereal is not available in ANY areas, because it's not real.
But wouldn't it be awesome to start each day with Rockhead and Scissorlegz? Mmmm . . . marshmallows.

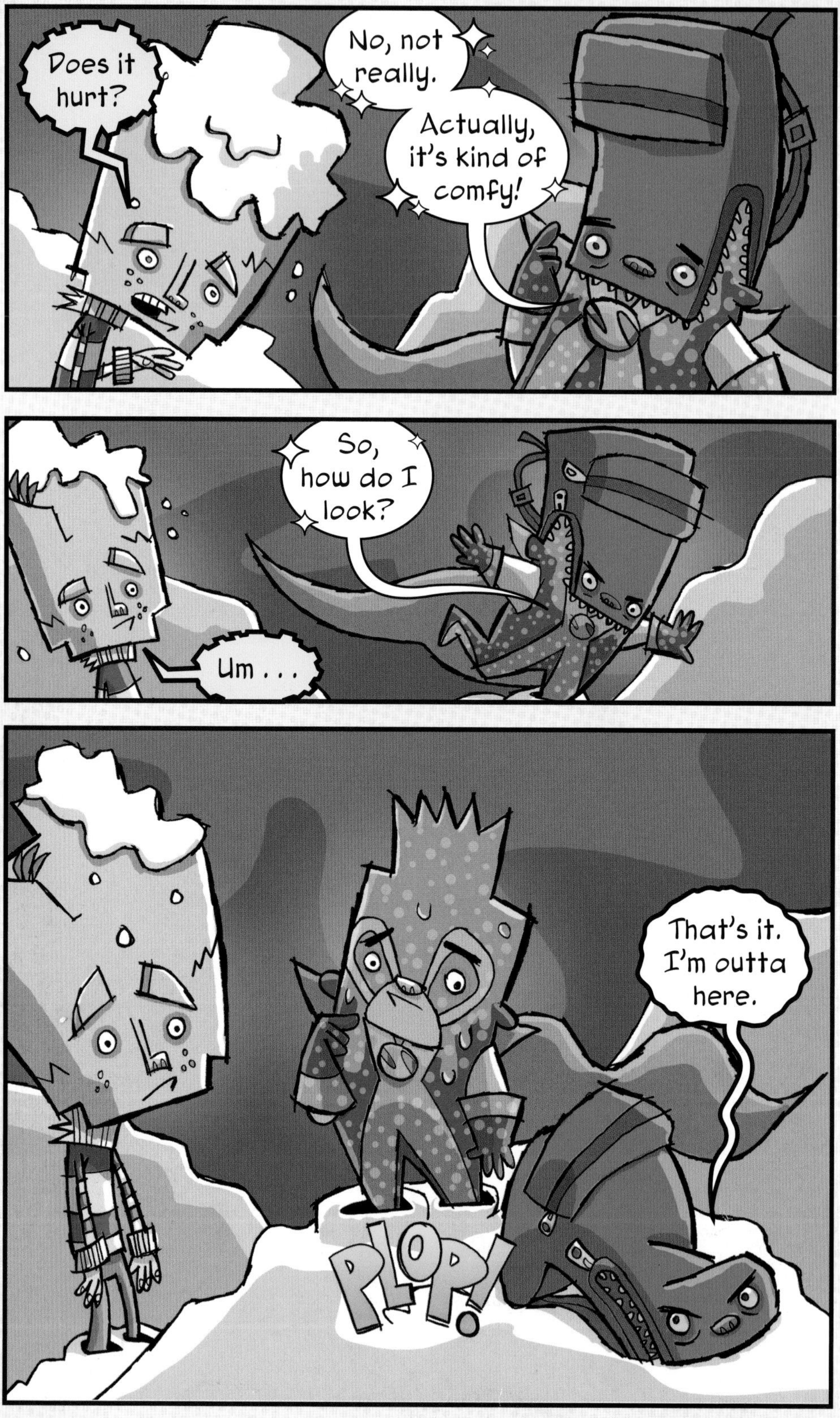
Does it hurt?
No, not really.
Actually, it's kind of comfy!
So, how do I look?
Um . . .
That's it. I'm outta here.
PLOP!

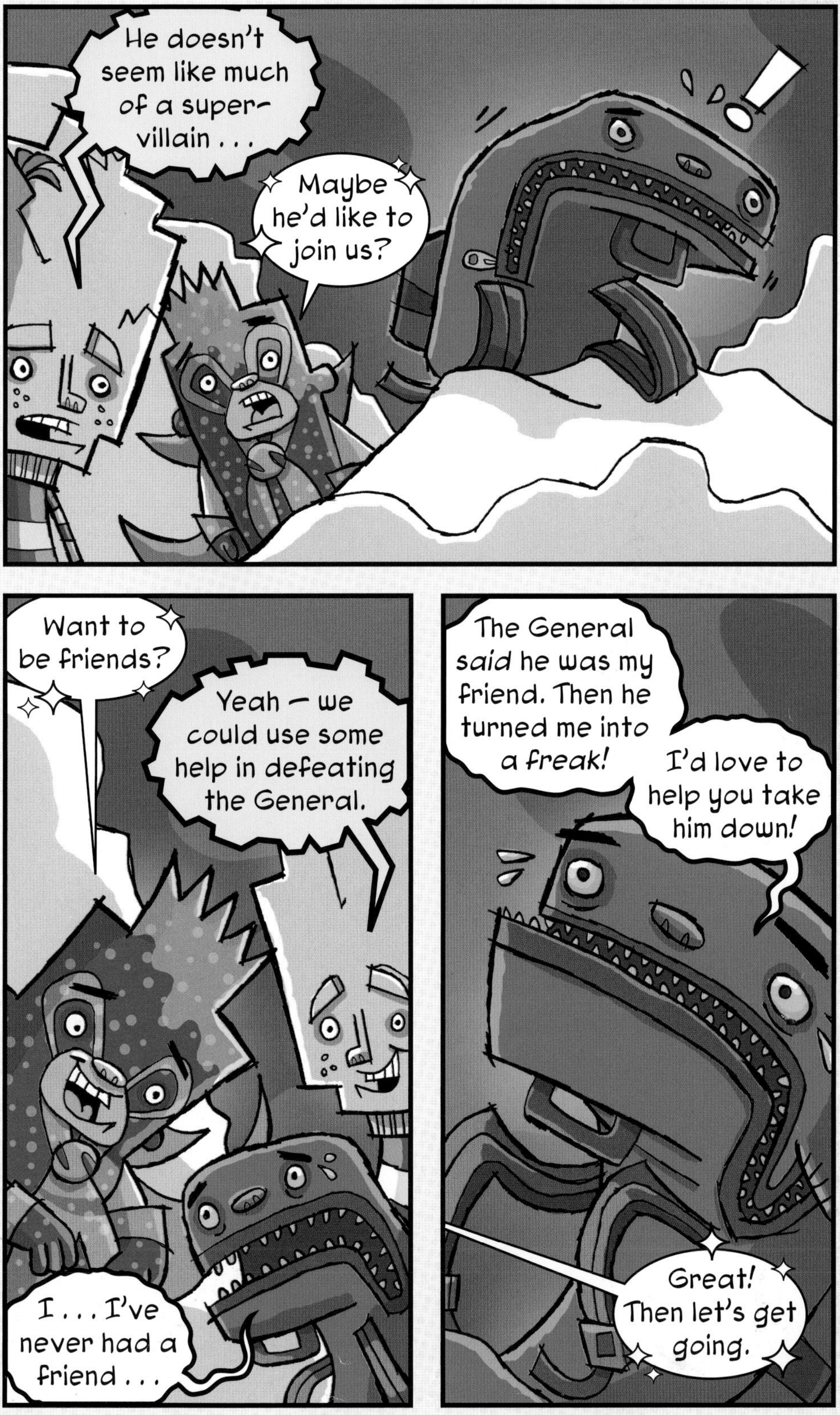
He doesn't seem like much of a super-villain . . .
Maybe he'd like to join us?
Want to be friends?
Yeah — we could use some help in defeating the General.
I . . . I've never had a friend . . .
The General *said* he was my friend. Then he turned me into a *freak!*
I'd love to help you take him down!
Great! Then let's get going.

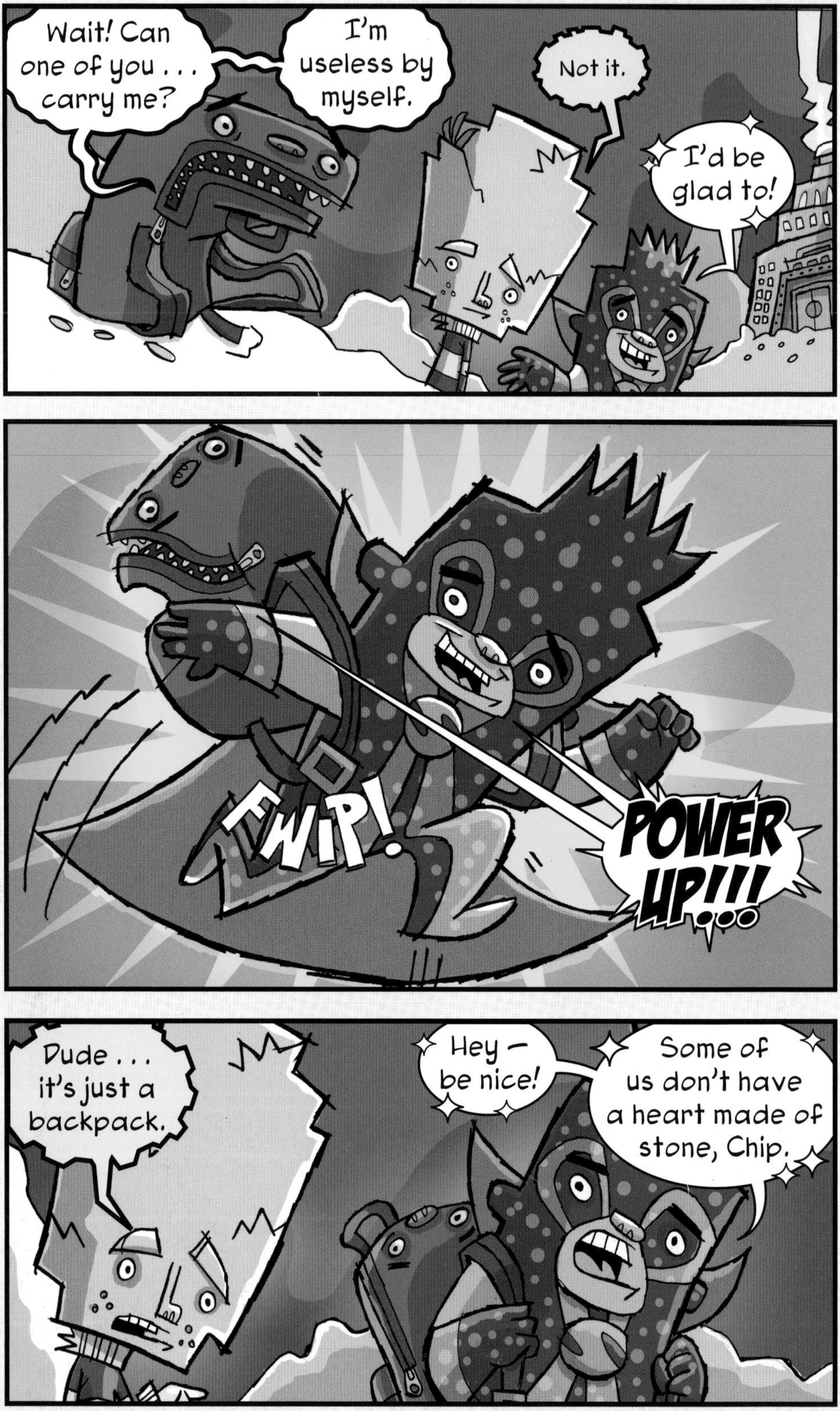
Wait! Can one of you . . . carry me?
I'm useless by myself.
Not it.
I'd be glad to!
FWIP!
POWER UP!!!
Dude . . . it's just a backpack.
Hey — be nice!
Some of us don't have a heart made of stone, Chip.

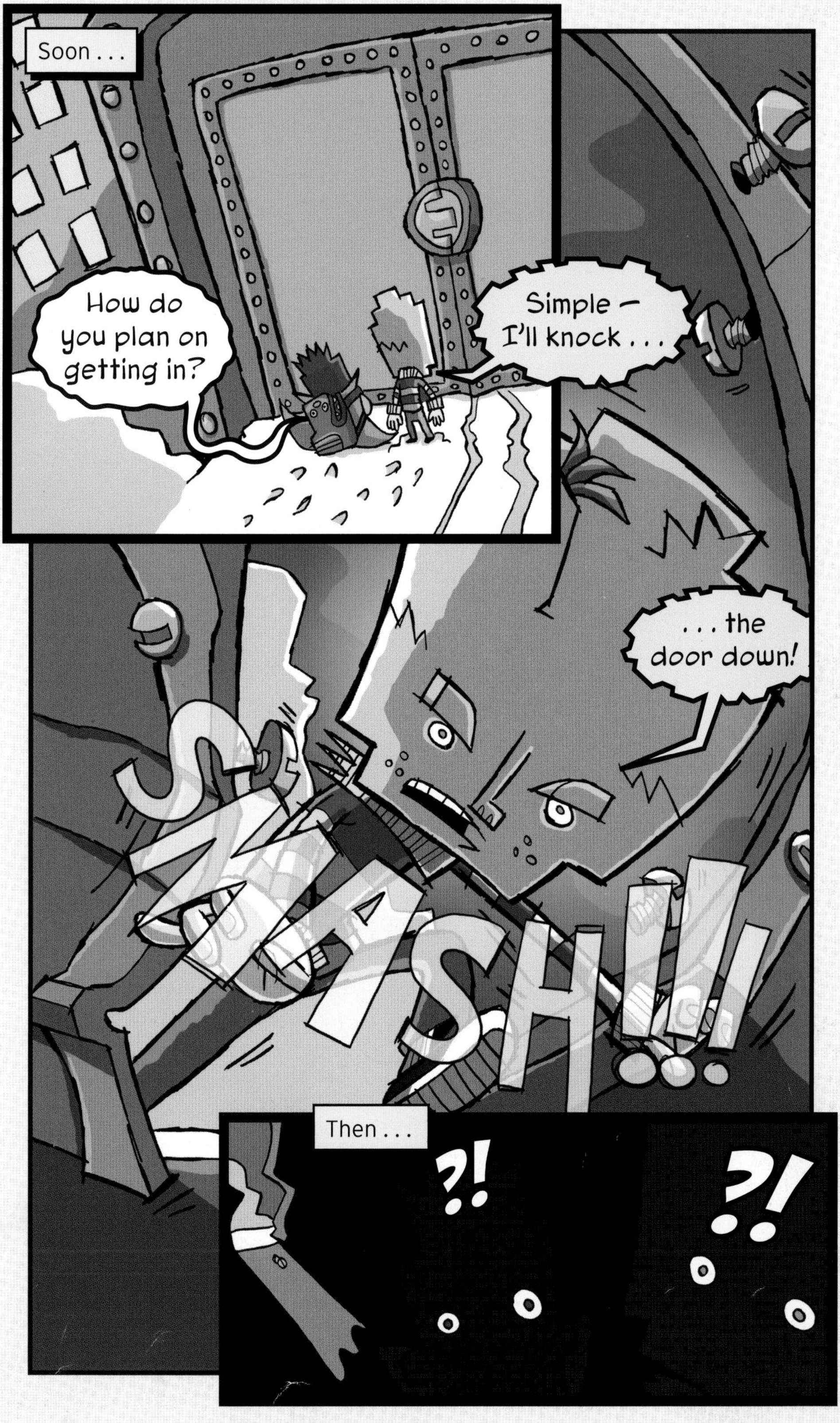
Soon . . .
How do you plan on getting in?
Simple — I'll knock . . .
. . . the door down!
SMASH!!!
Then . . .
?!
?!

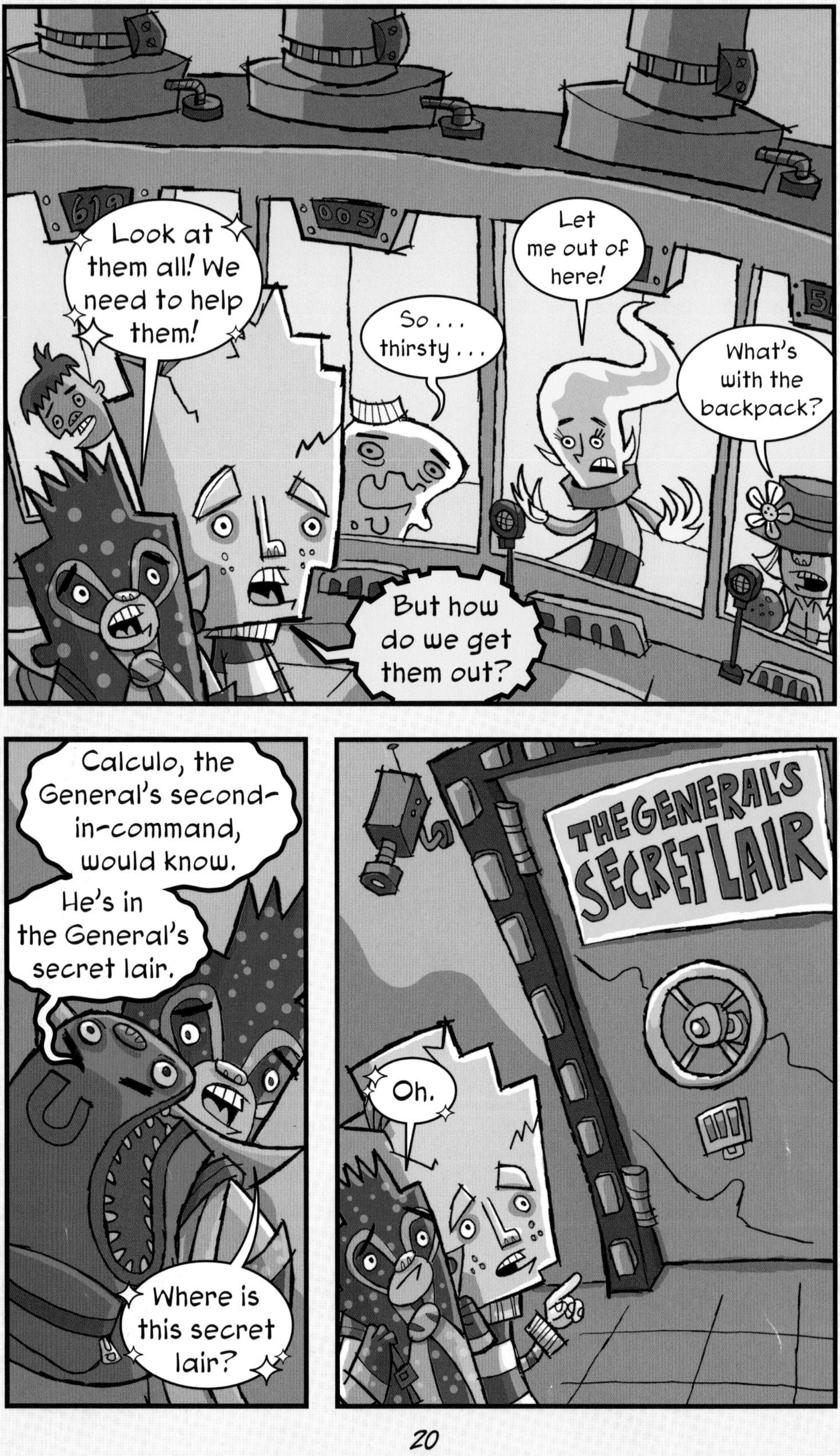
Look at them all! We need to help them!
So . . . thirsty . . .
Let me out of here!
What's with the backpack?
But how do we get them out?
Calculo, the General's second-in-command, would know.
He's in the General's secret lair.
Where is this secret lair?
THE GENERAL'S SECRET LAIR
Oh.

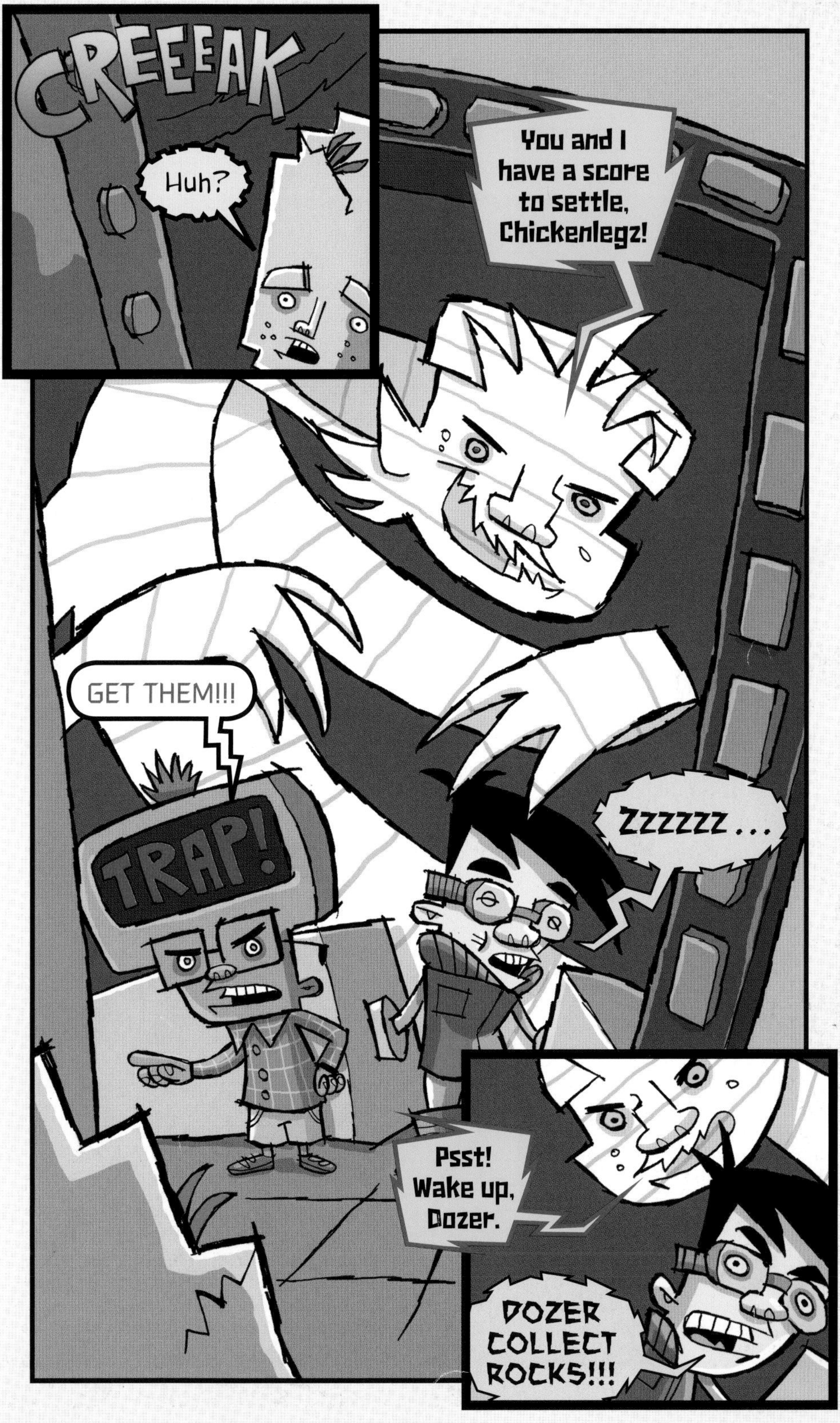
CREEEAK
Huh?
You and I have a score to settle, Chickenlegz!
GET THEM!!!
TRAP!
Zzzzzz . . .
Psst! Wake up, Dozer.
DOZER COLLECT ROCKS!!!

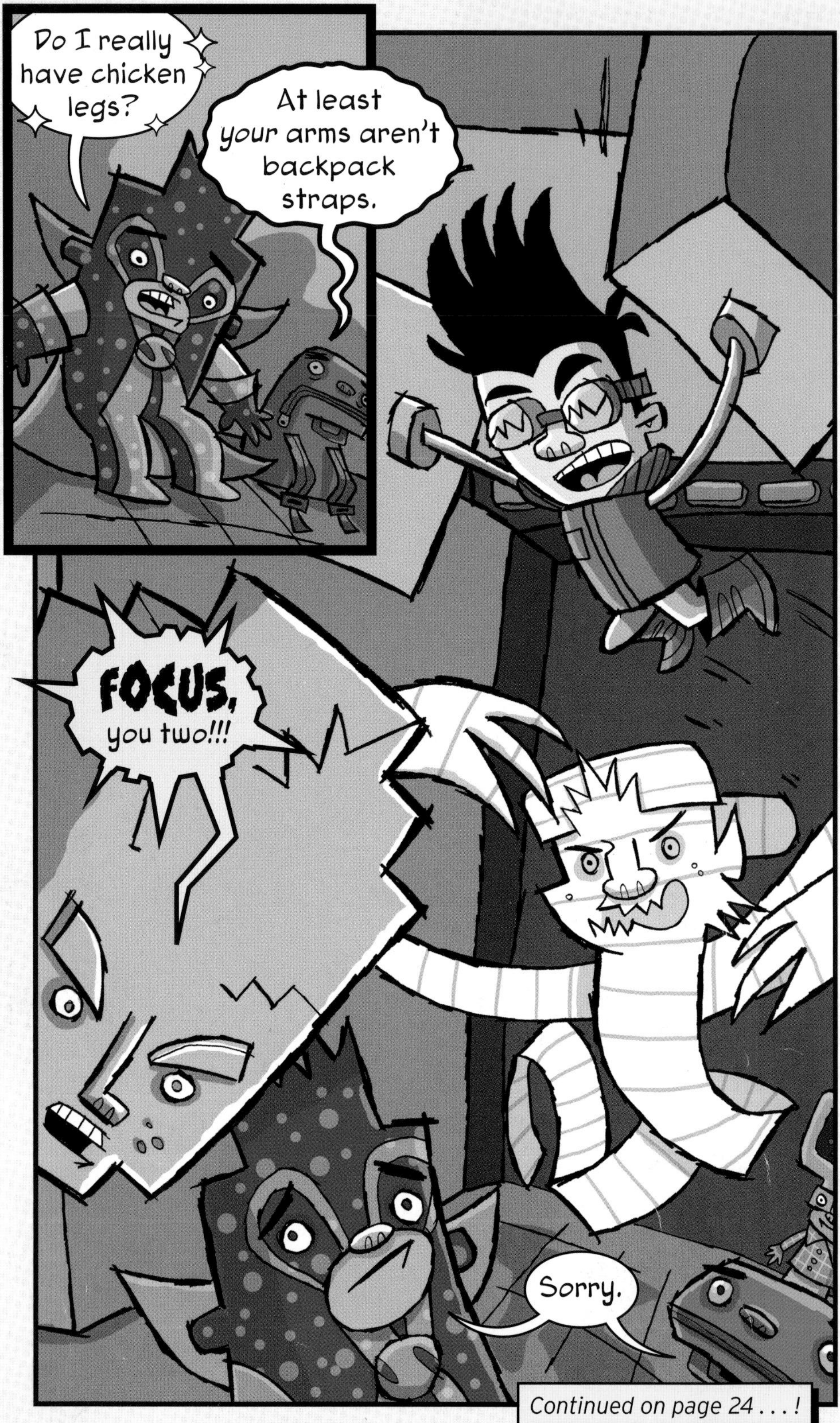
Do I really have chicken legs?
At least your arms aren't backpack straps.
FOCUS, you two!!!
Sorry.

Continued on page 24 . . . !

ADVERTISEMENT

LOOK, KIDS! STICKERS!

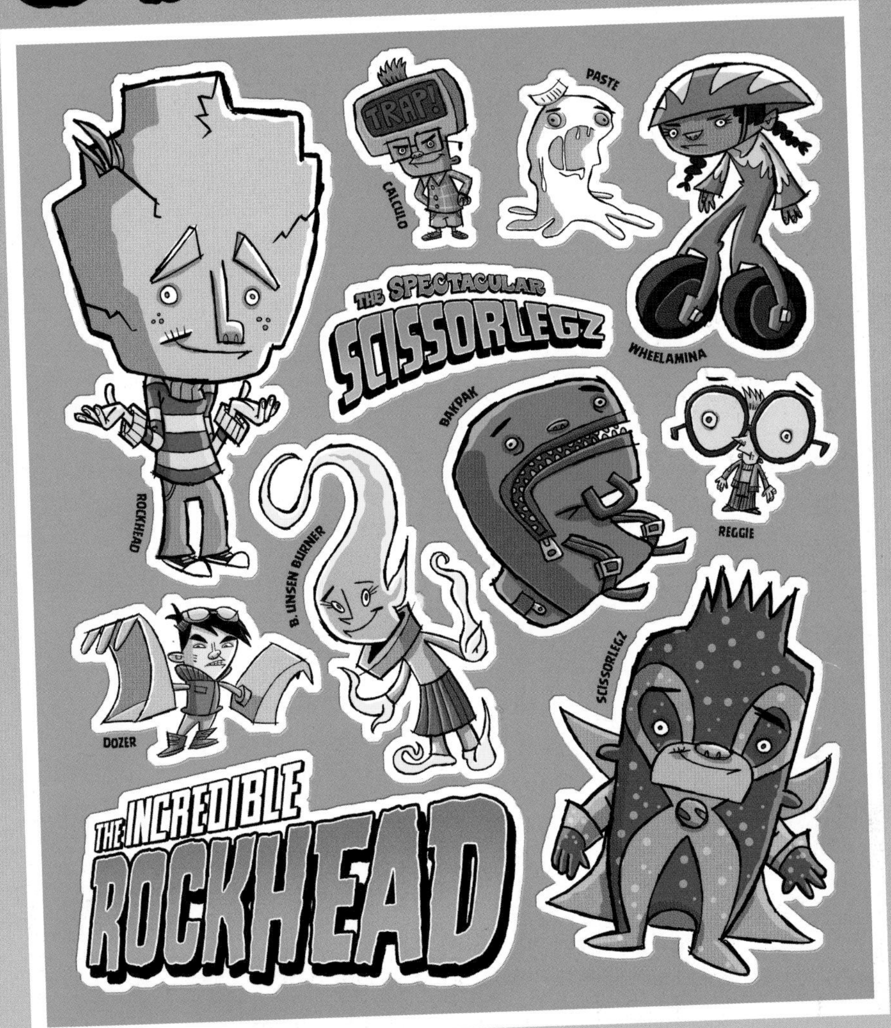

TRAP!
CALCULO
PASTE
WHEELAMINA
THE SPECTACULAR SCISSORLEGZ
BAKPAK
REGGIE
ROCKHEAD
B. UNSEN BURNER
SCISSORLEGZ
DOZER
THE INCREDIBLE ROCKHEAD

COLLECT THEM ALL! ONLY $1.00!*

YES! Please rush me a sheet of stickers today!

NAME *Nerdy Lab Sidekick*

ADDRESS *Secret Headquarters*

CITY/STATE/ZIP *Top Secret*

*Price per sheet. Characters may vary. Most of the time you'll probably get doubles of Reggie. LAME! If you're lucky, you'll get a limited edition Scissorlegz puffy sticker! Stickers should not be adhered to walls, floors, your sister, dogs, cats, dinnerware, cars, or valuables.

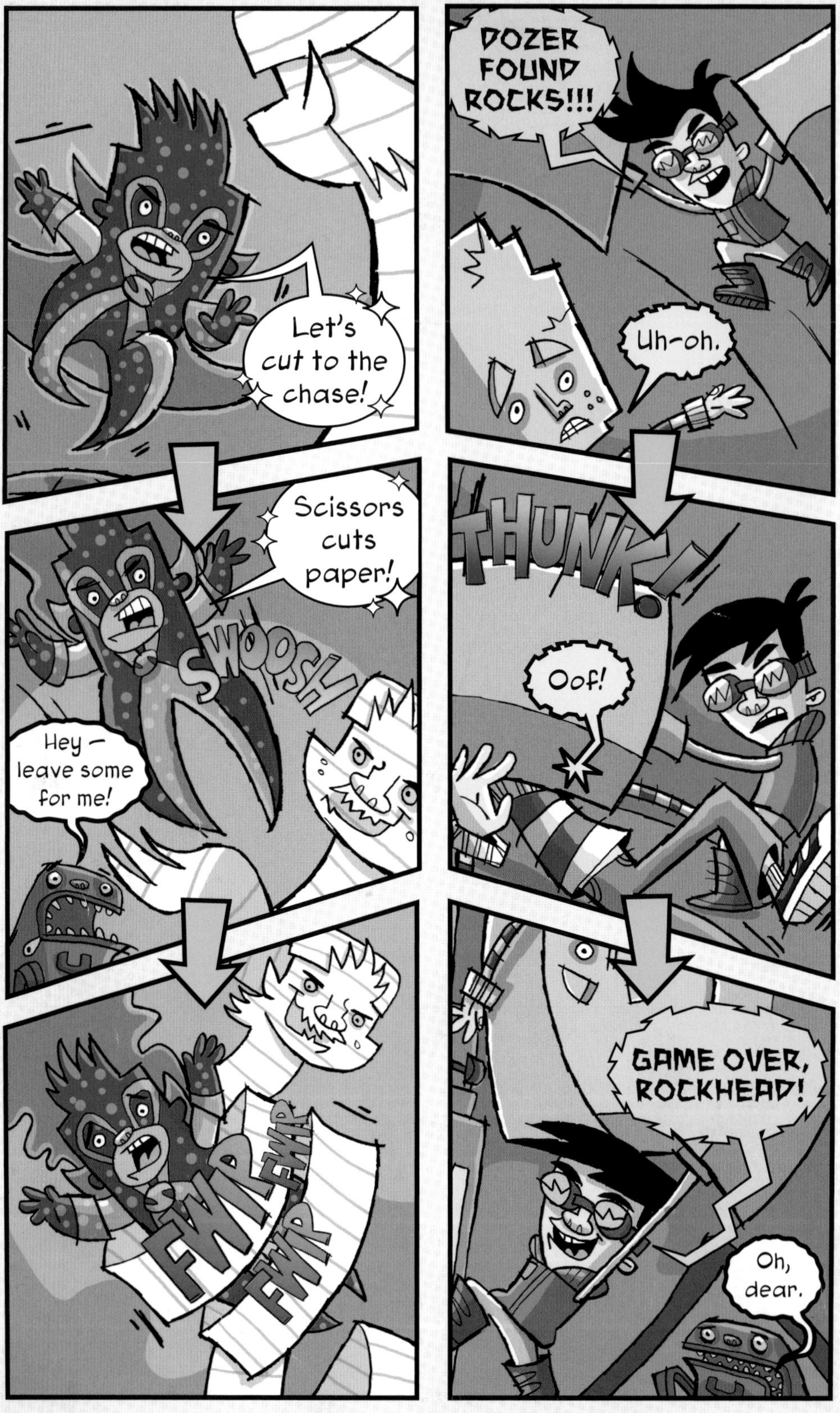
Let's cut to the chase!
Scissors cuts paper!
SWOOSH
Hey — leave some for me!
FWIP FWIP FWIP
DOZER FOUND ROCKS!!!
Uh-oh.
THUNK!
Oof!
GAME OVER, ROCKHEAD!
Oh, dear.

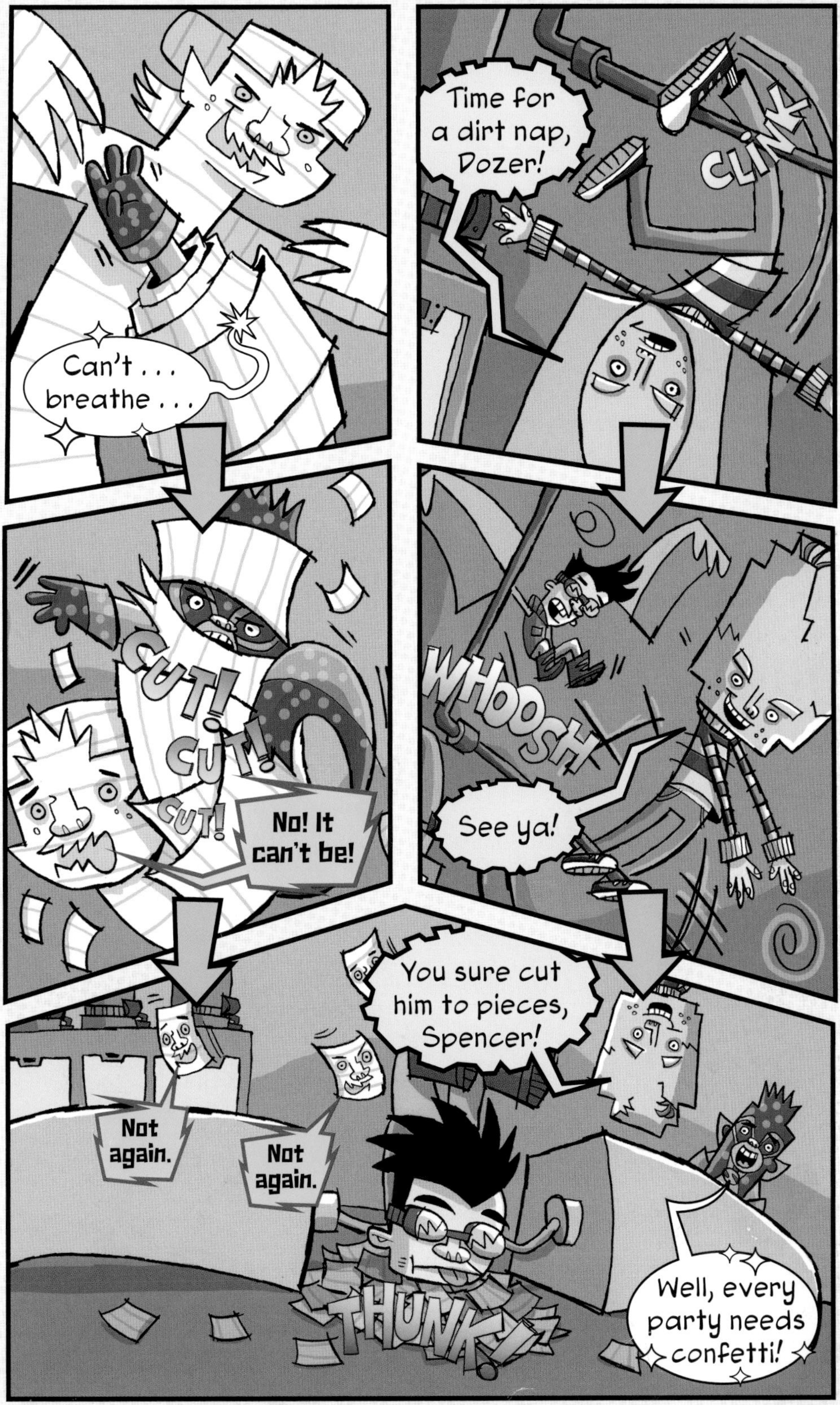
Can't . . . breathe . . .
Time for a dirt nap, Dozer!
CLINK
CUT! CUT! CUT!
No! It can't be!
WHOOSH
See ya!
Not again.
Not again.
You sure cut him to pieces, Spencer!
THUNK!
Well, every party needs confetti!

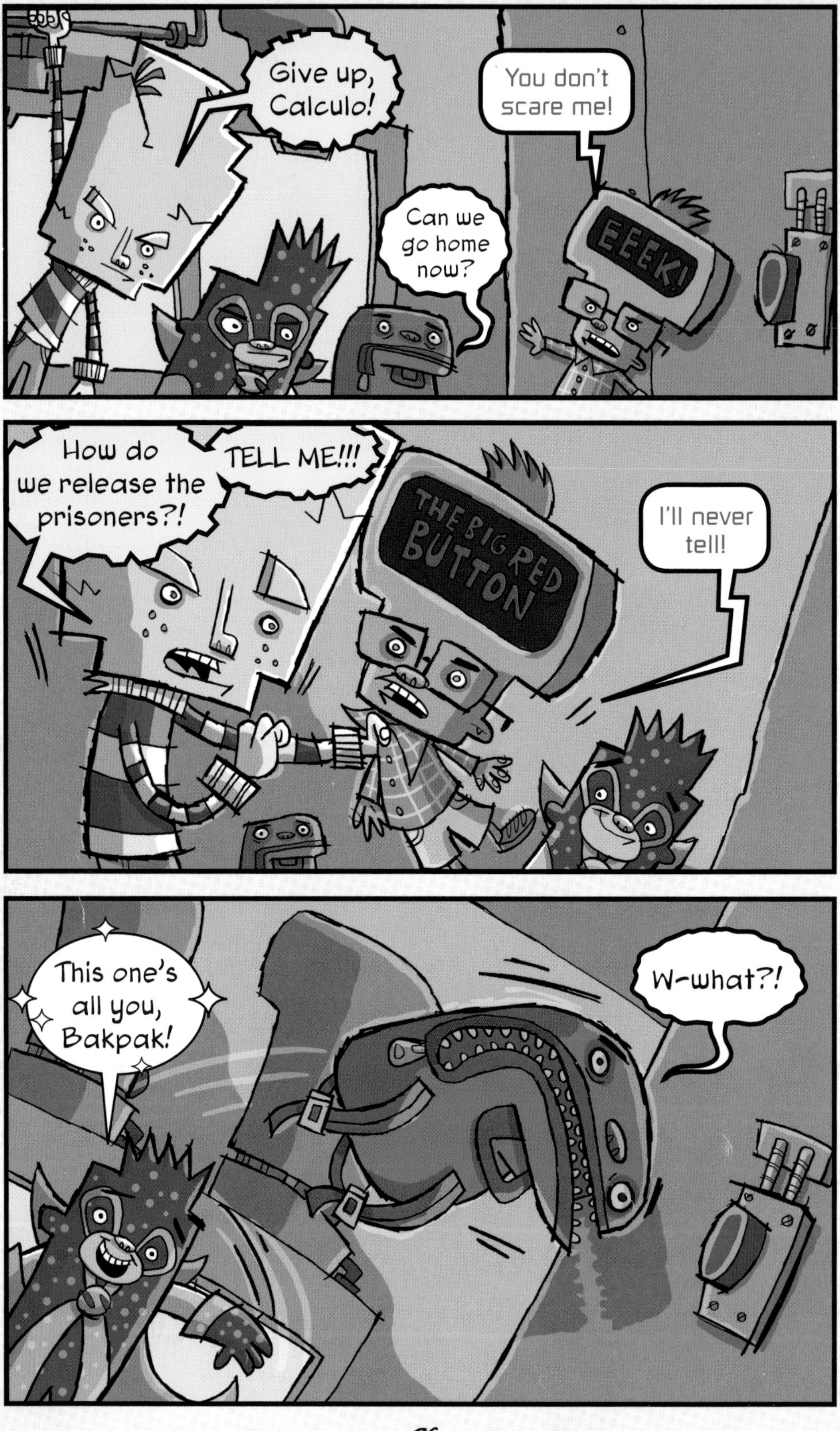
Give up, Calculo!
You don't scare me!
Can we go home now?
EEEK!
How do we release the prisoners?!
TELL ME!!!
THE BIG RED BUTTON
I'll never tell!
This one's all you, Bakpak!
W-what?!

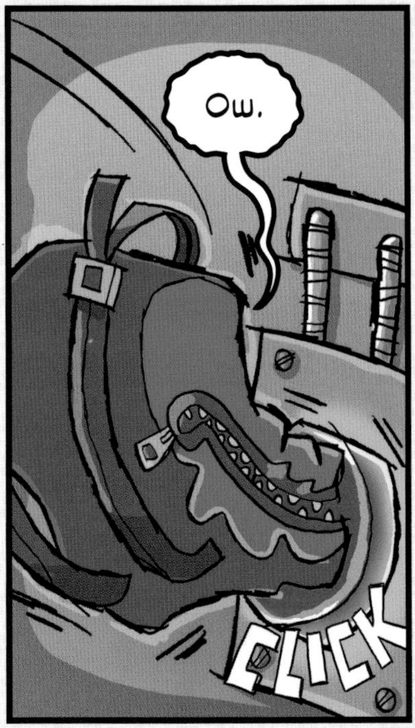
Ow.
CLICK

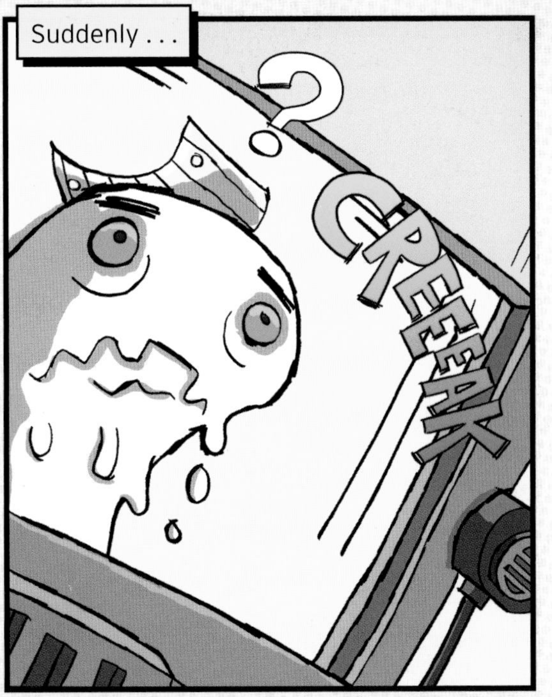
Suddenly . . .
?
CREEEAK

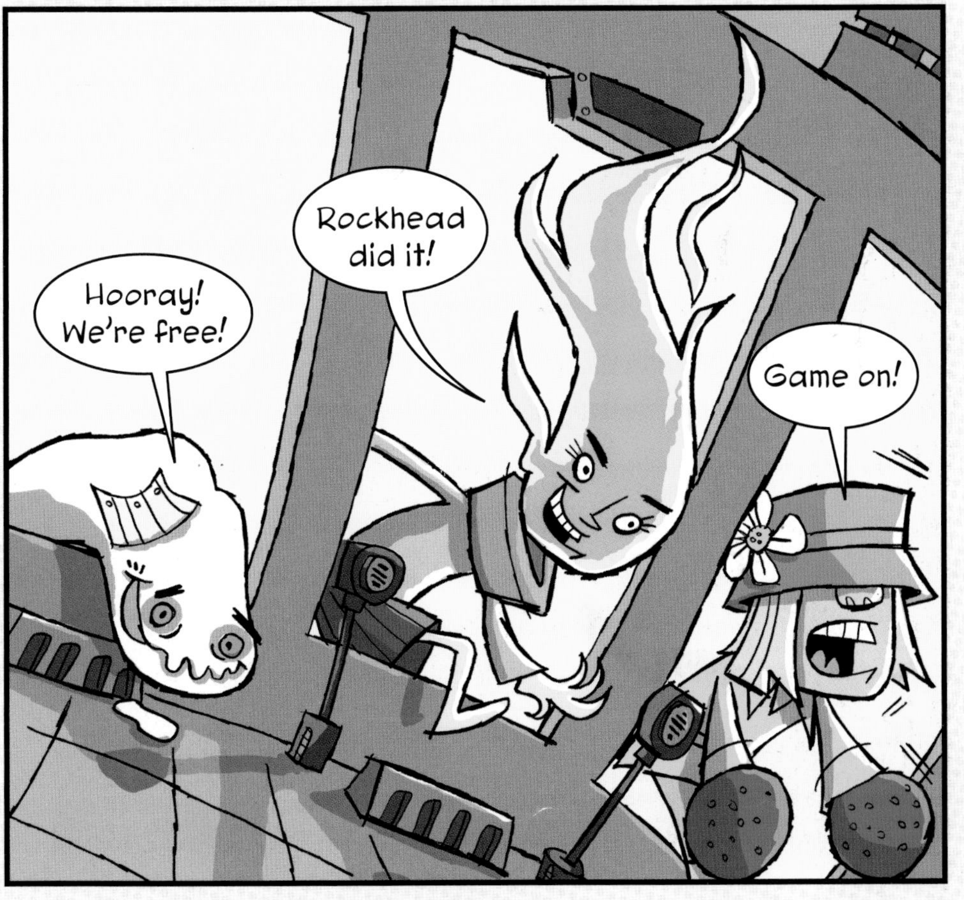
Hooray! We're free!
Rockhead did it!
Game on!

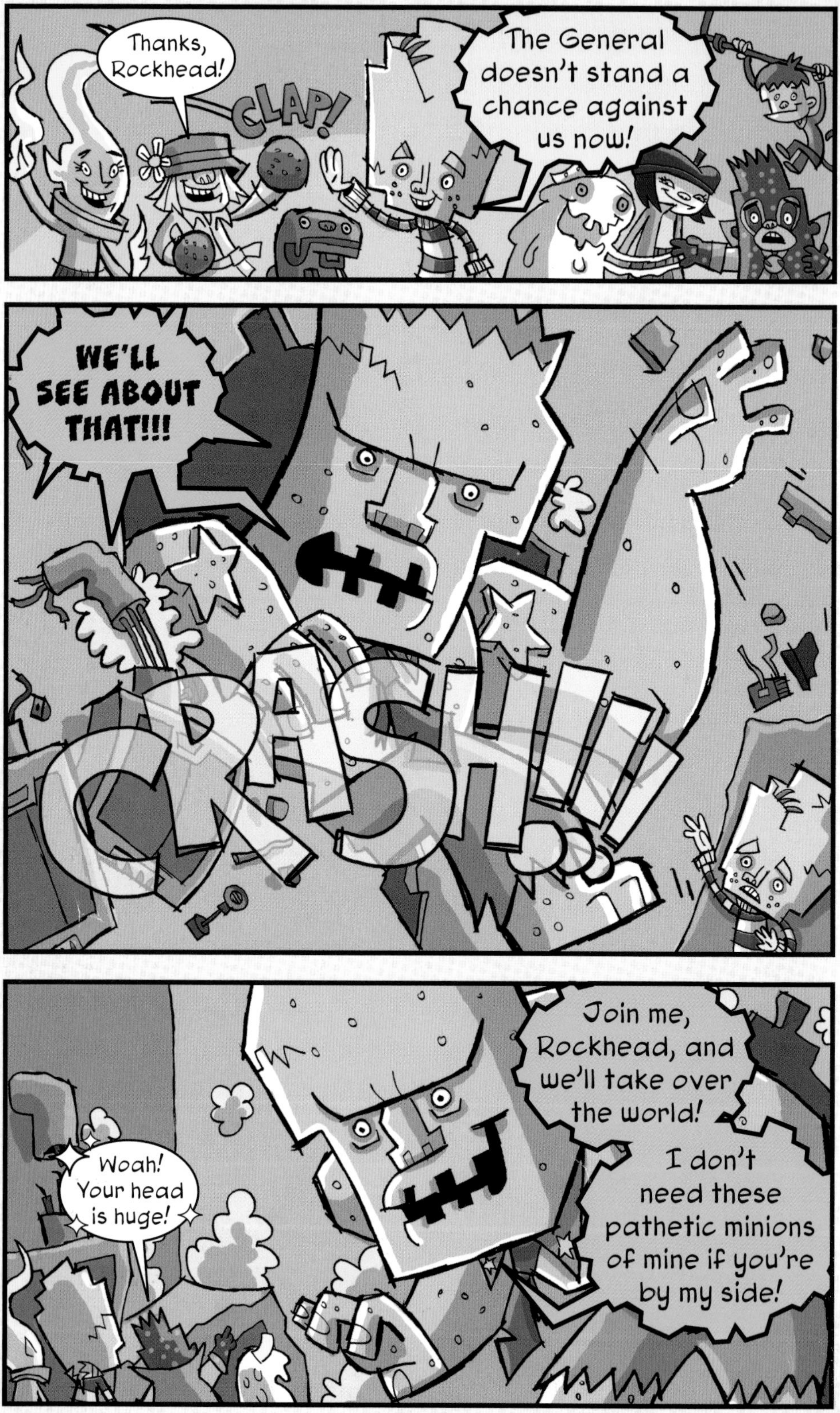
Thanks, Rockhead!
CLAP!
The General doesn't stand a chance against us now!
WE'LL SEE ABOUT THAT!!!
CRASH!!
Join me, Rockhead, and we'll take over the world!
I don't need these pathetic minions of mine if you're by my side!
Woah! Your head is huge!

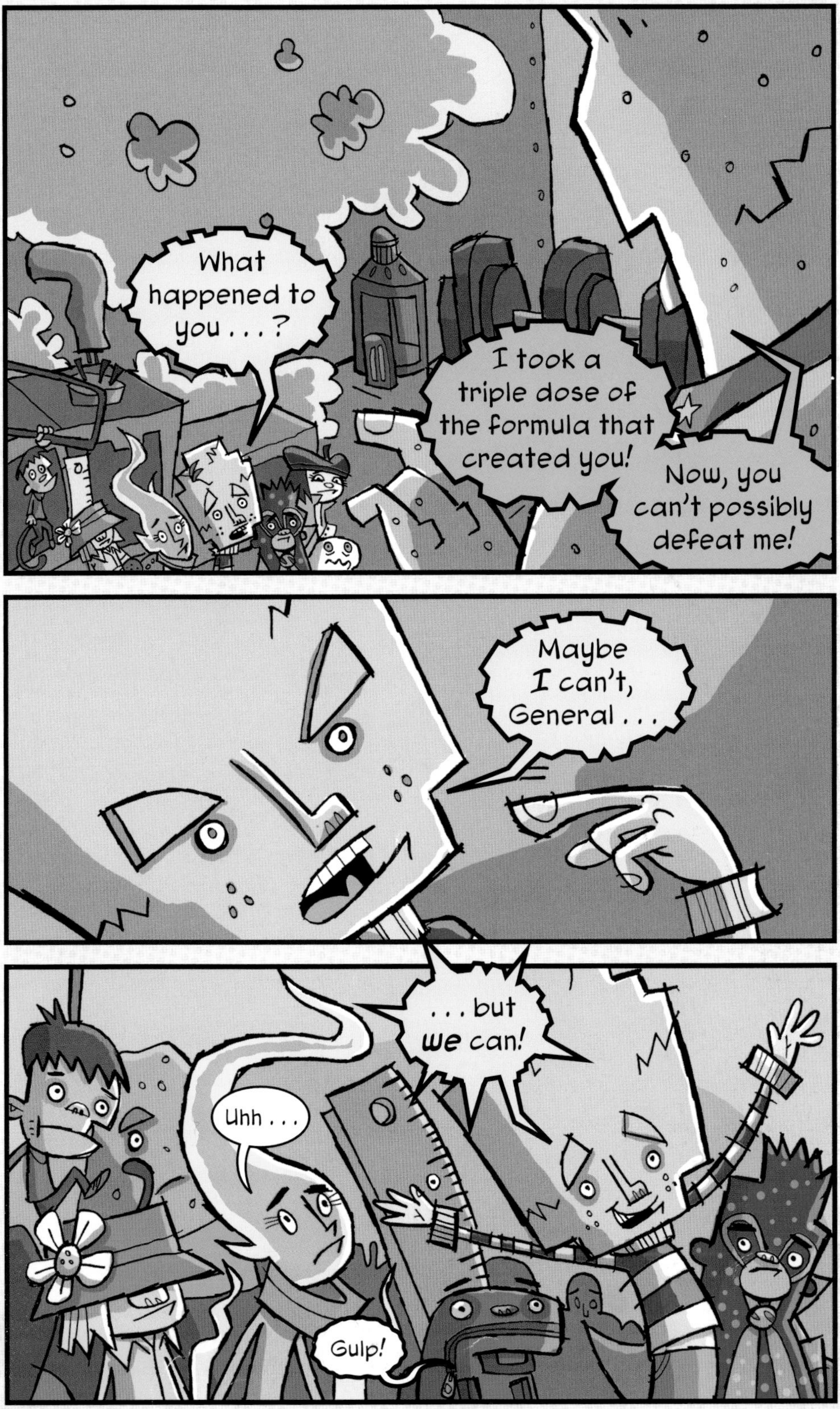
What happened to you . . . ?
I took a triple dose of the formula that created you!
Now, you can't possibly defeat me!
Maybe I can't, General . . .
. . . but we can!
Uhh . . .
Gulp!

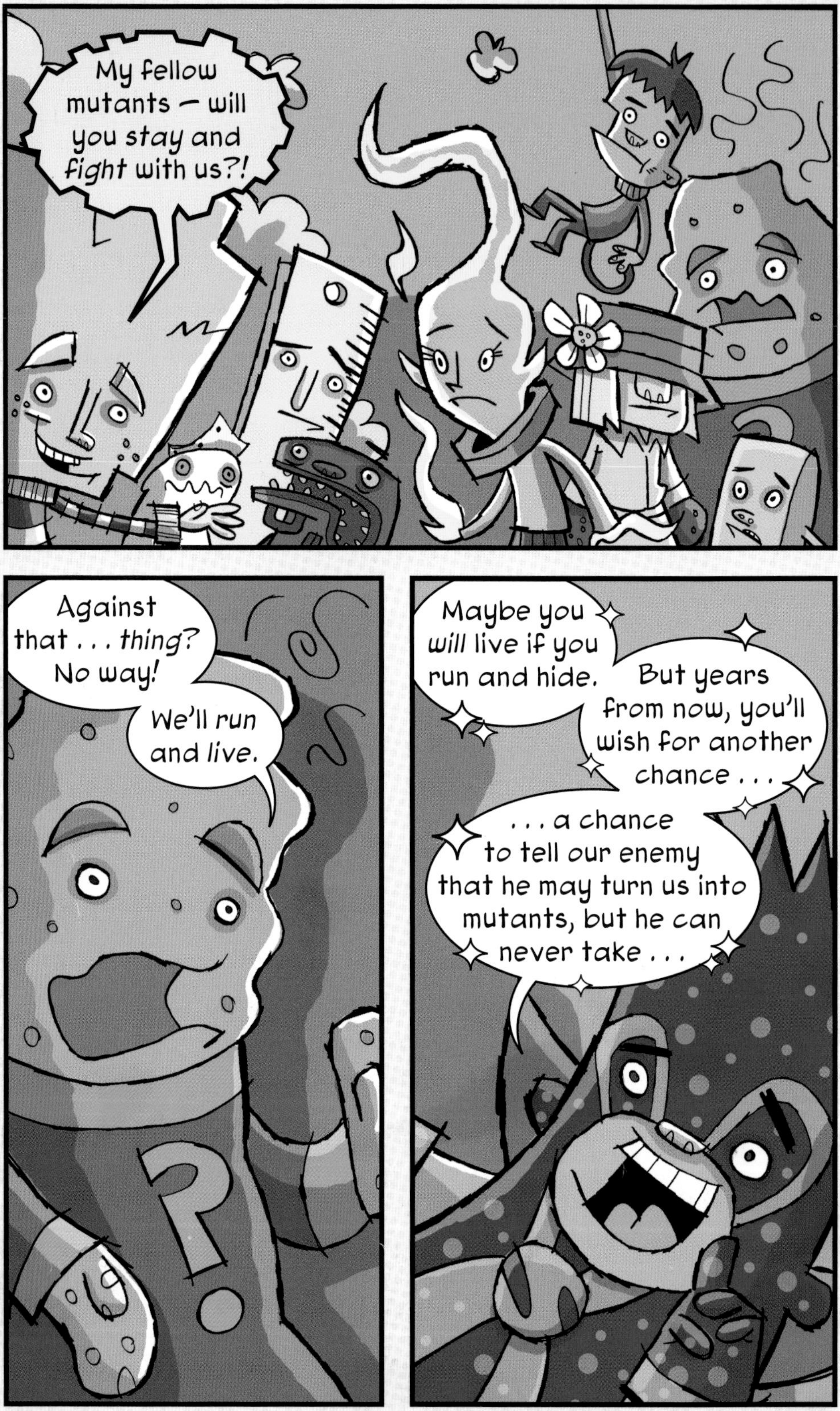
My fellow mutants — will you stay and fight with us?!
Against that . . . thing? No way!
We'll run and live.
Maybe you will live if you run and hide.
But years from now, you'll wish for another chance . . .
. . . a chance to tell our enemy that he may turn us into mutants, but he can never take . . .

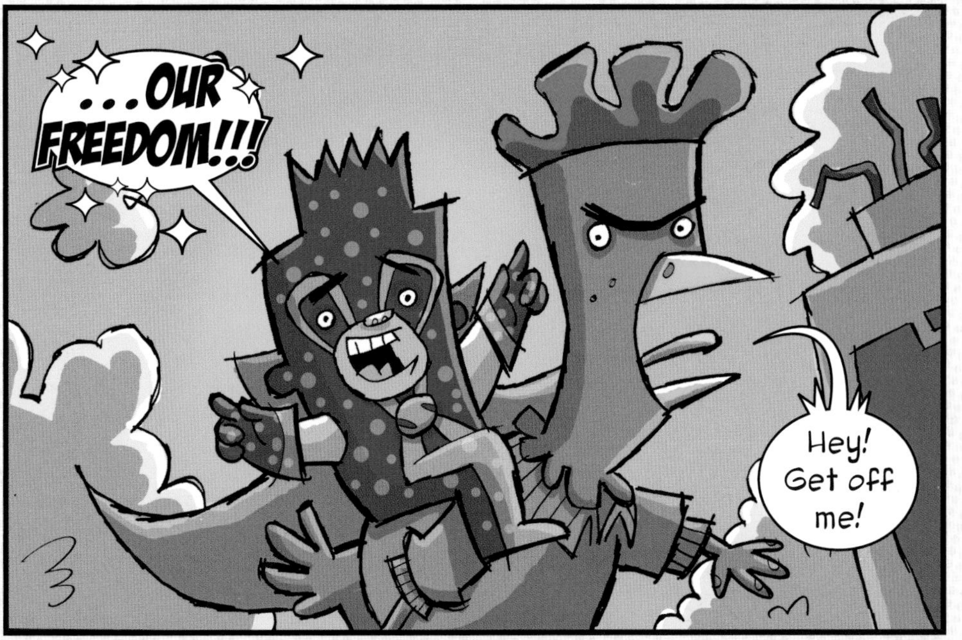
...OUR FREEDOM!!!
Hey! Get off me!

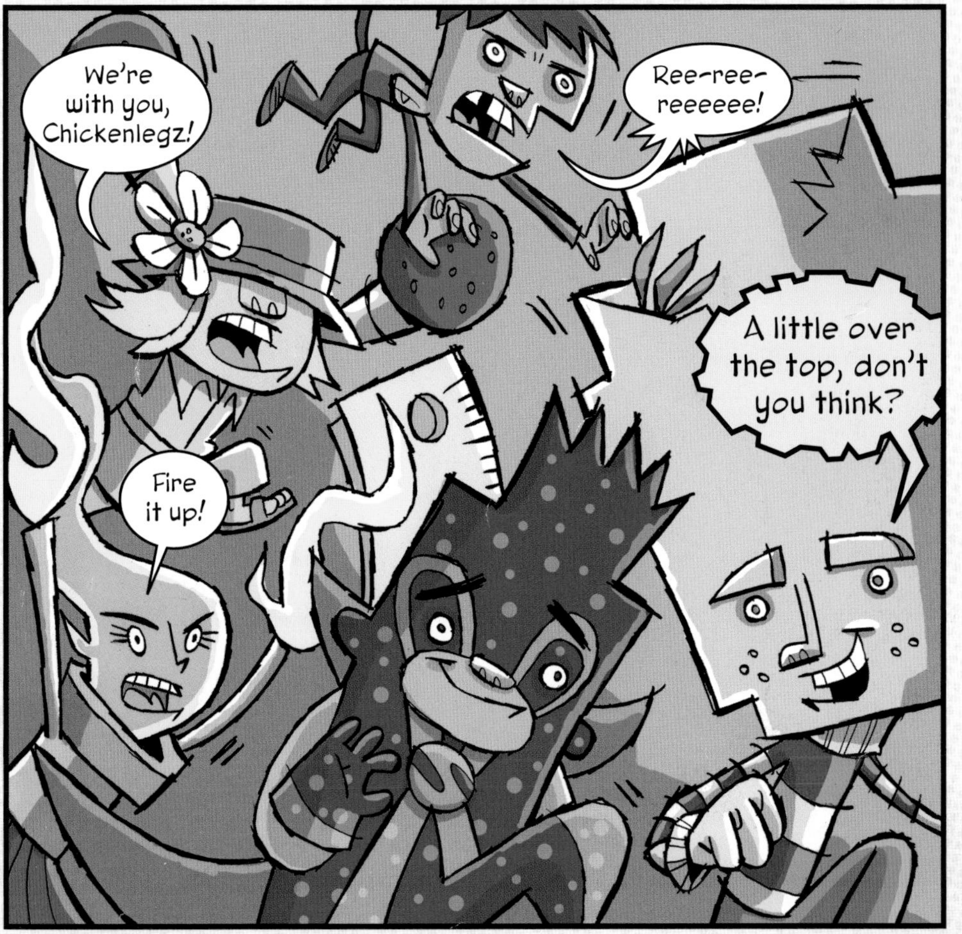
We're with you, Chickenlegz!
Ree-ree-reeeeee!
A little over the top, don't you think?
Fire it up!

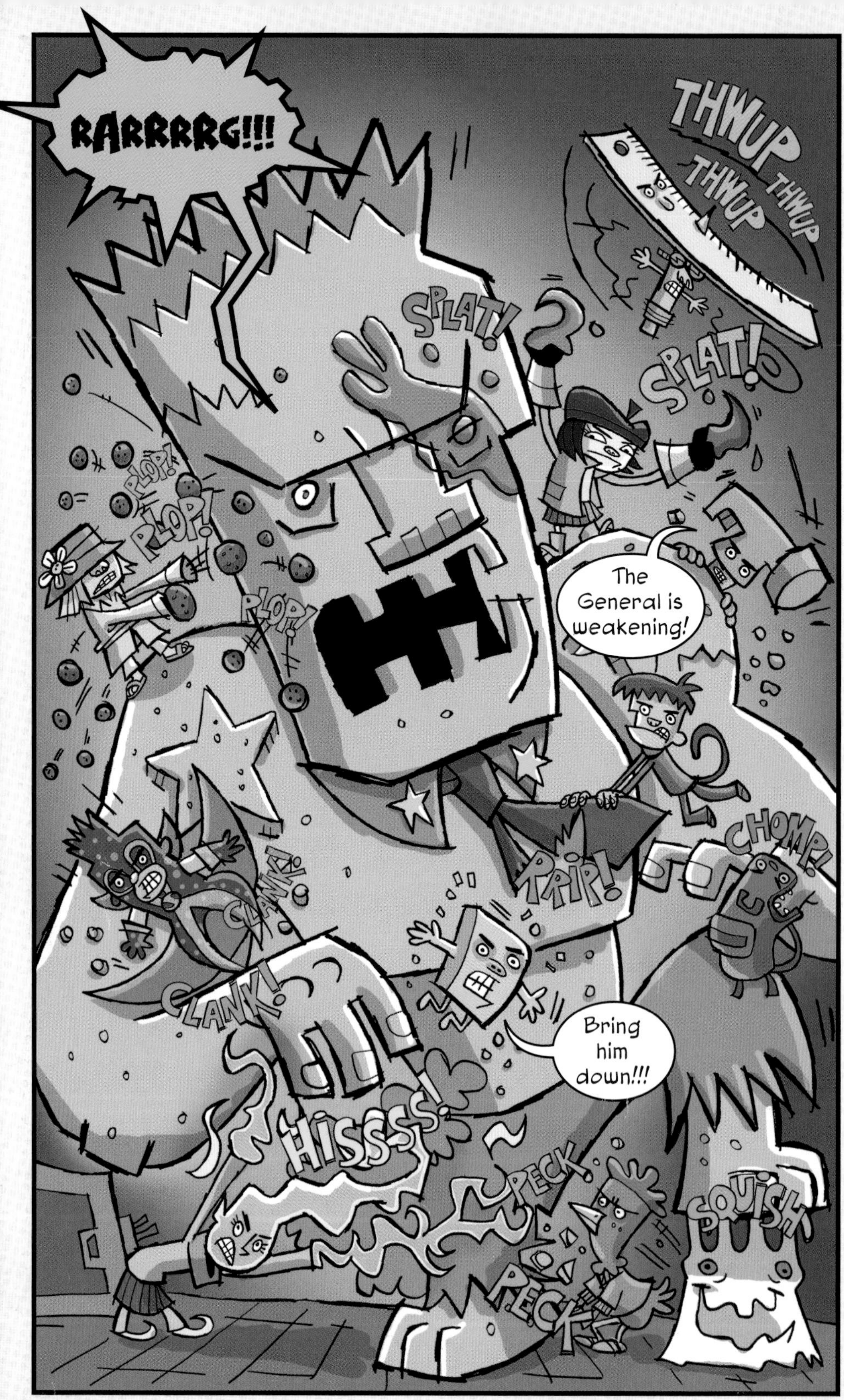
RARRRRG!!!
THWUP THWUP THWUP
SPLAT!
SPLAT!
PLOP!
PLOP!
PLOP!
The General is weakening!
CHOMP!
RRIP!
CLANK!
CLANK!
Bring him down!!!
HISSSS!
PECK
PECK
SQUISH

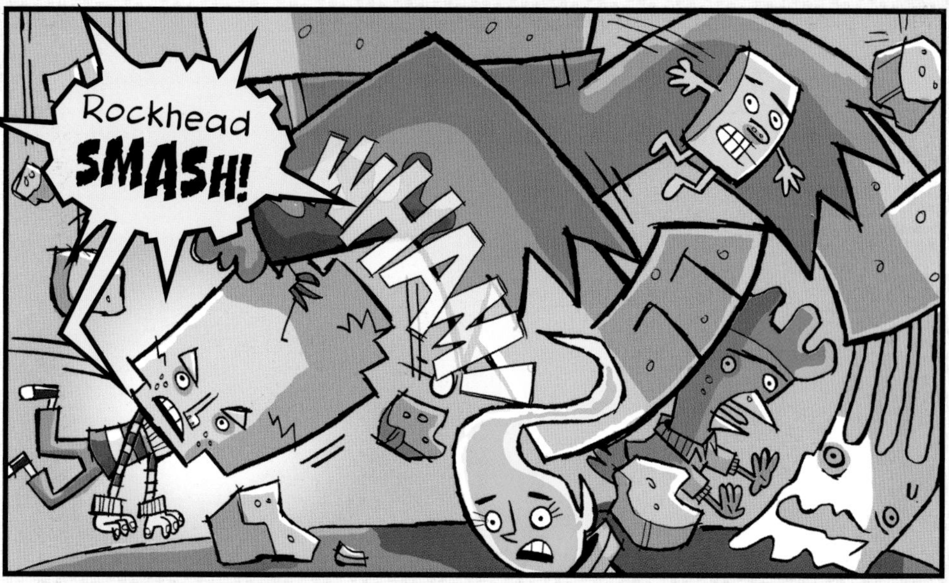
Rockhead SMASH!
WHAM!

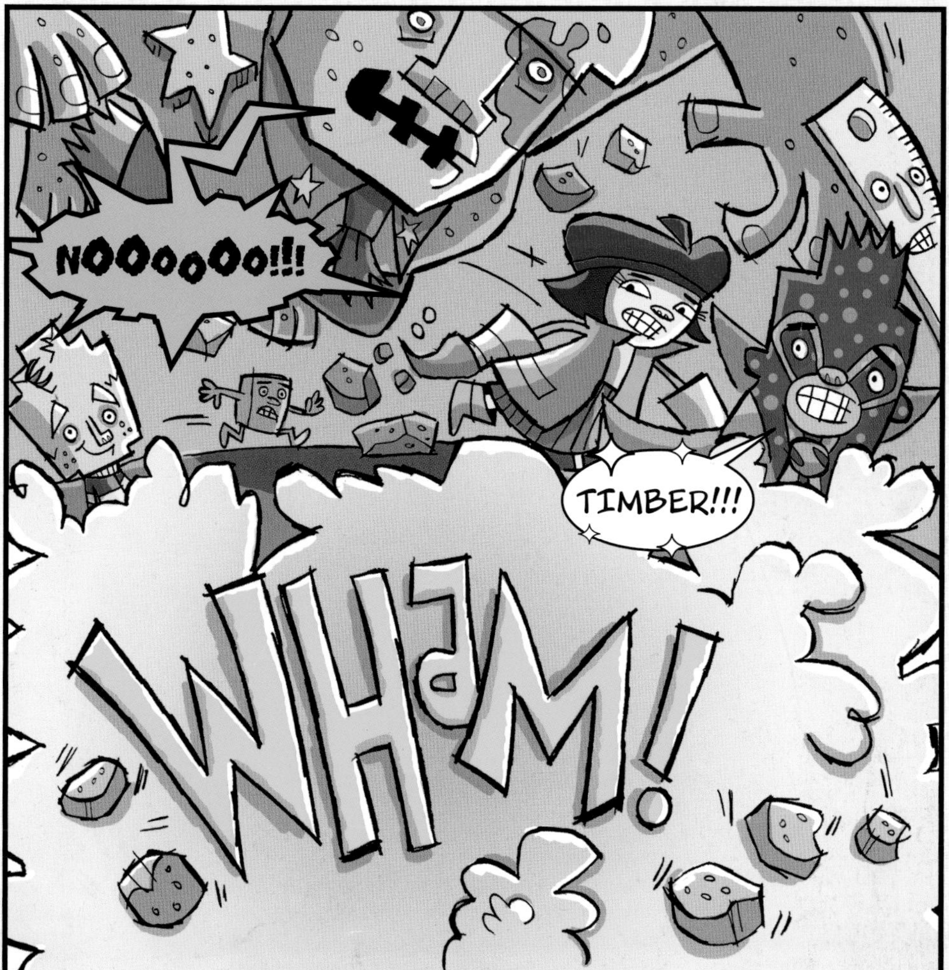
NOOooOOo!!!
TIMBER!!!
WHAM!

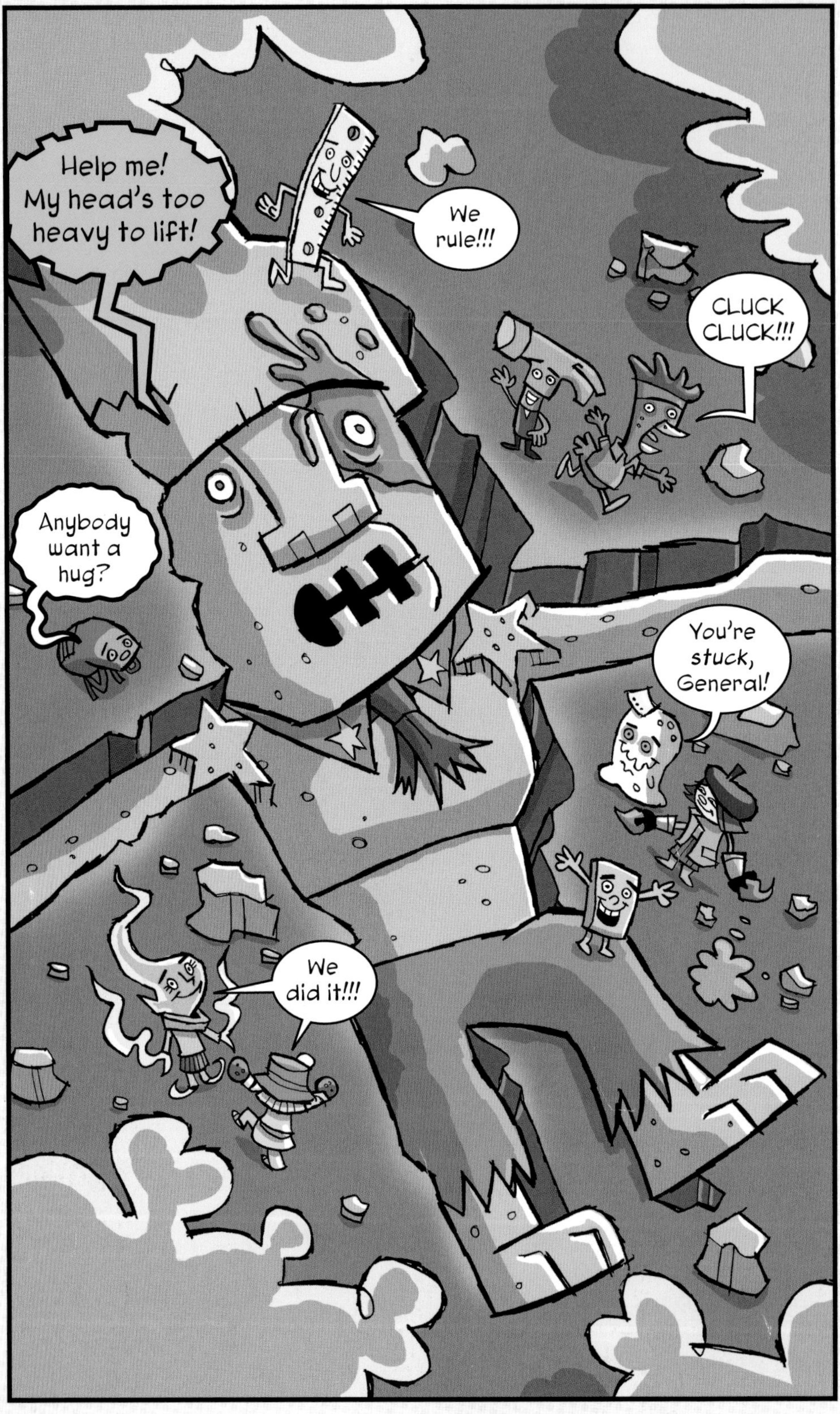
Help me! My head's too heavy to lift!
We rule!!!
CLUCK CLUCK!!!
Anybody want a hug?
You're stuck, General!
We did it!!!

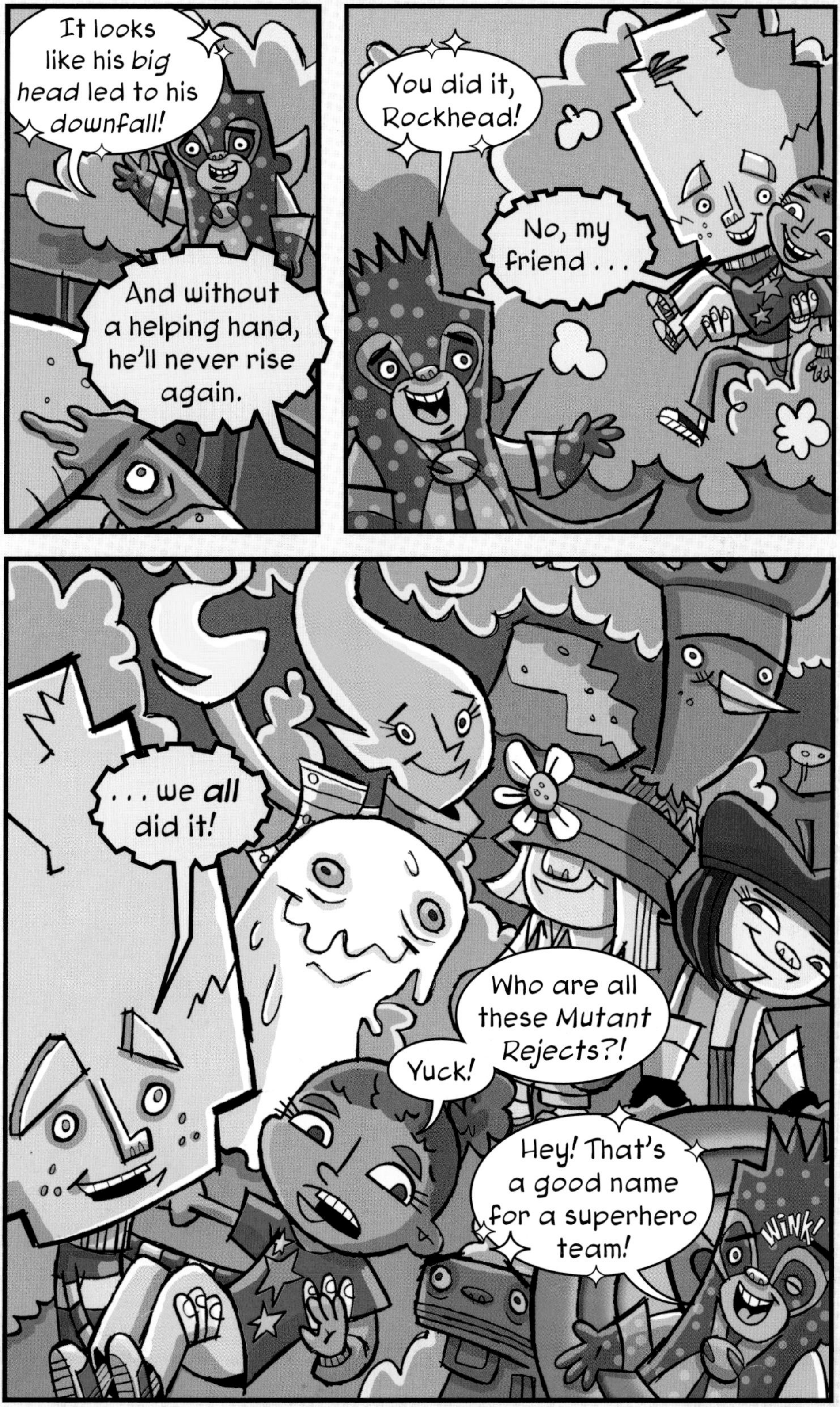
It looks like his *big head* led to his *downfall!*
And without a helping hand, he'll never rise again.
You did it, Rockhead!
No, my friend . . .
. . . we *all* did it!
Yuck!
Who are all these Mutant Rejects?!
Hey! That's a good name for a superhero team!
WINK!

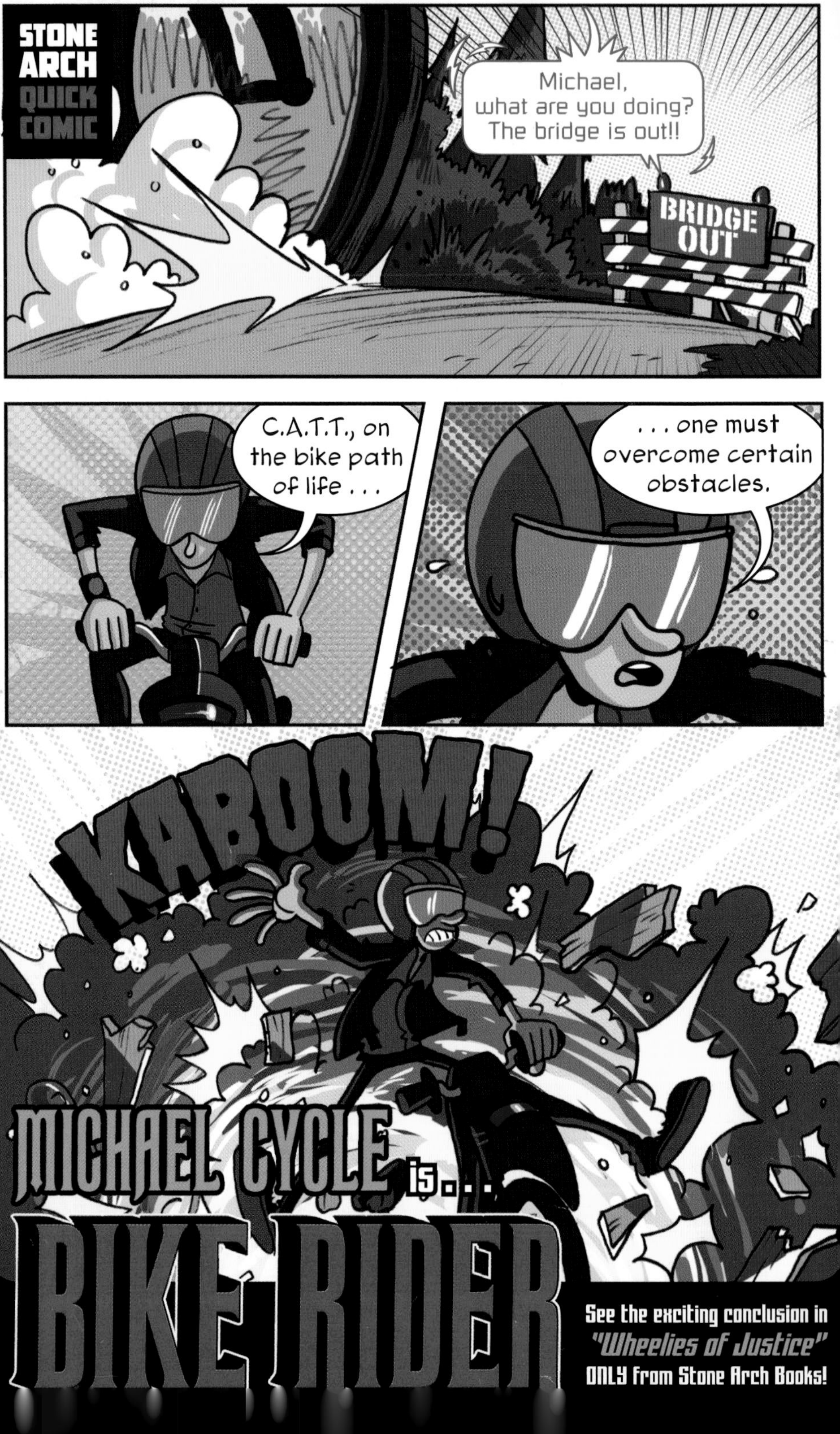

STONE ARCH QUICK COMIC
Michael, what are you doing? The bridge is out!!
BRIDGE OUT
C.A.T.T., on the bike path of life . . .
. . . one must overcome certain obstacles.
KABOOM!
MICHAEL CYCLE is . . .
BIKE RIDER
See the exciting conclusion in "Wheelies of Justice" ONLY from Stone Arch Books!

FROM THE DESK OF STONE ARCH BOOKS:

MEET THE CREATORS!

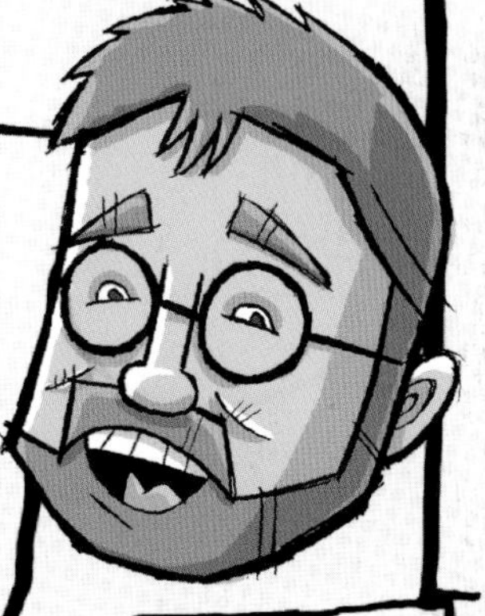

SCOTT NICKEL - AUTHOR

Scott Nickel works by day at Paws, inc., Jim Davis's famous Garfield studio, and he freelances by night. Scott has created hundreds of humorous greeting cards and written several children's books, short fiction for *Boys' Life* magazine, comic strips, and lots of really funny knock-knock jokes. Scott currently lives in Indiana with his wife, two sons, six cats, and several sea monkeys.

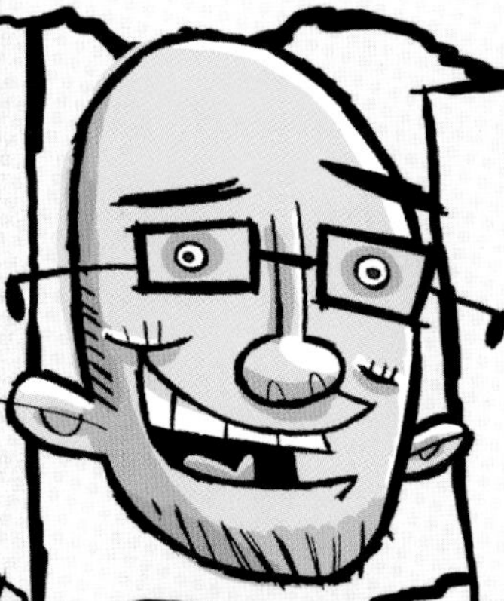

C.S. JENNINGS - ILLUSTRATOR

C.S. Jennings has been a freelance illustrator for over a decade. Jennings has created caricatures, editorial cartoons, greeting cards, t-shirt art, logos, children's books, card games — you name it. He also wrote and illustrated the children's picture book *Animal Band*. In 1994, he won an Addy Award for his work in advertising. He currently lives in Austin, Texas.

SEAN TULIEN - WRITER

Sean Tulien is a children's book editor living and working in Minnesota. In his spare time, he likes to eat sushi, exercise outdoors, listen to loud music, read comics, play with his evil hamster, Beatrice, and write books like this one.

DONALD LEMKE - WRITER

Donald Lemke works as a children's book editor. He is the author of the Zinc Alloy graphic novel adventure series. He also wrote *Captured Off Guard*, a World War II story, and a graphic novelization of Gulliver's Travels, both of which were selected by the Junior Library Guild.

DO YOU LIKE THIS BOOK? HAVE A FAVORITE CHARACTER?

WRITE TO US ABOUT IT: STONE ARCH BOOKS 7825 Telegraph Road, Minneapolis, MN 55438

HEY KIDS! IT'S TIME AGAIN FOR...

THE GLOSSARY

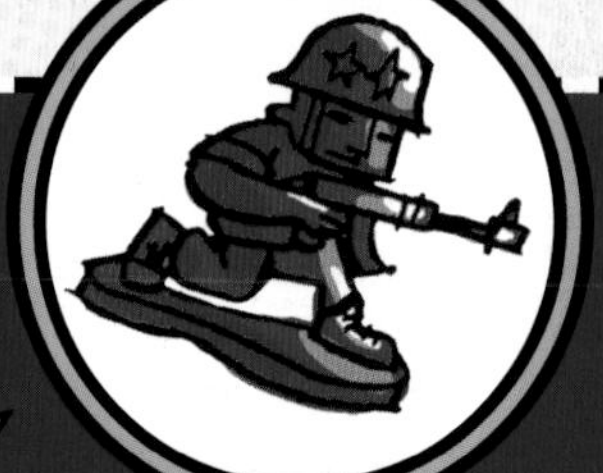

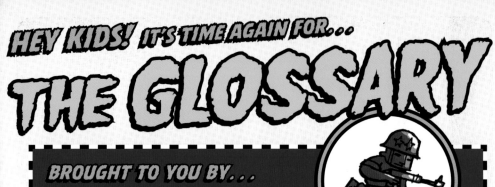

BROUGHT TO YOU BY... THE GENERAL'S LEAGUE OF EVIL MUTANTS!

experiment (ek-SPER-uh-ment)—a scientific test used to try out a theory, or to turn nerdy teens into mutants

formula (FOR-myuh-uh)—a recipe for something scientific, or a super-villain's evil serum

lair (LAIR)—a place where a wild animal rests and sleeps, or where an evil scientist performs experiments

mutant (MYOO-tuhnt)—a living thing who has undergone genetic changes, like Rockhead or that Bakpak weirdo

reject (REE-jekt)—someone who is cast out or thrown aside, or just not very cool at all

super-villain (SOO-pur-VIL-uhn)—an evil person. A super-villain is far more evil than an everyday villain.

useless (YOOSS-liss)—not capable of doing anything, just like Bakpak's weak, little arms

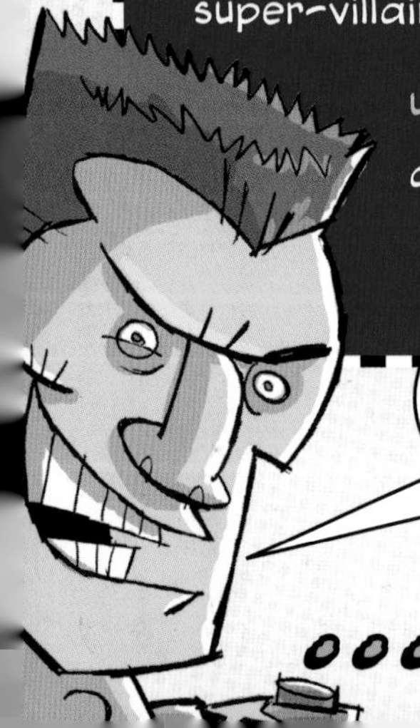
Welcome to my secret LAIR! Would you like to be my next MUTANT EXPERIMENT?

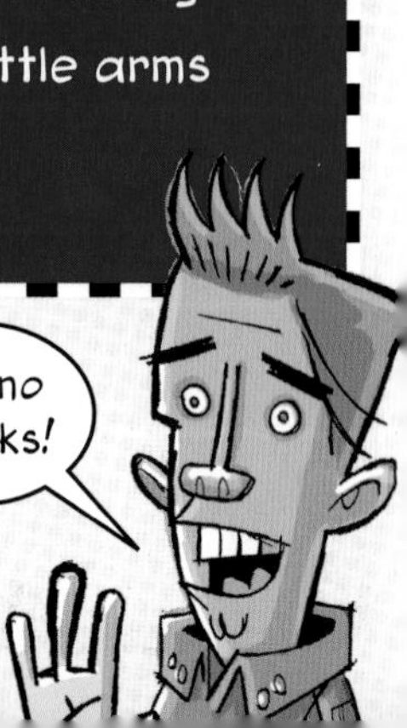
Um, no thanks!

...SIGN UP NOW!

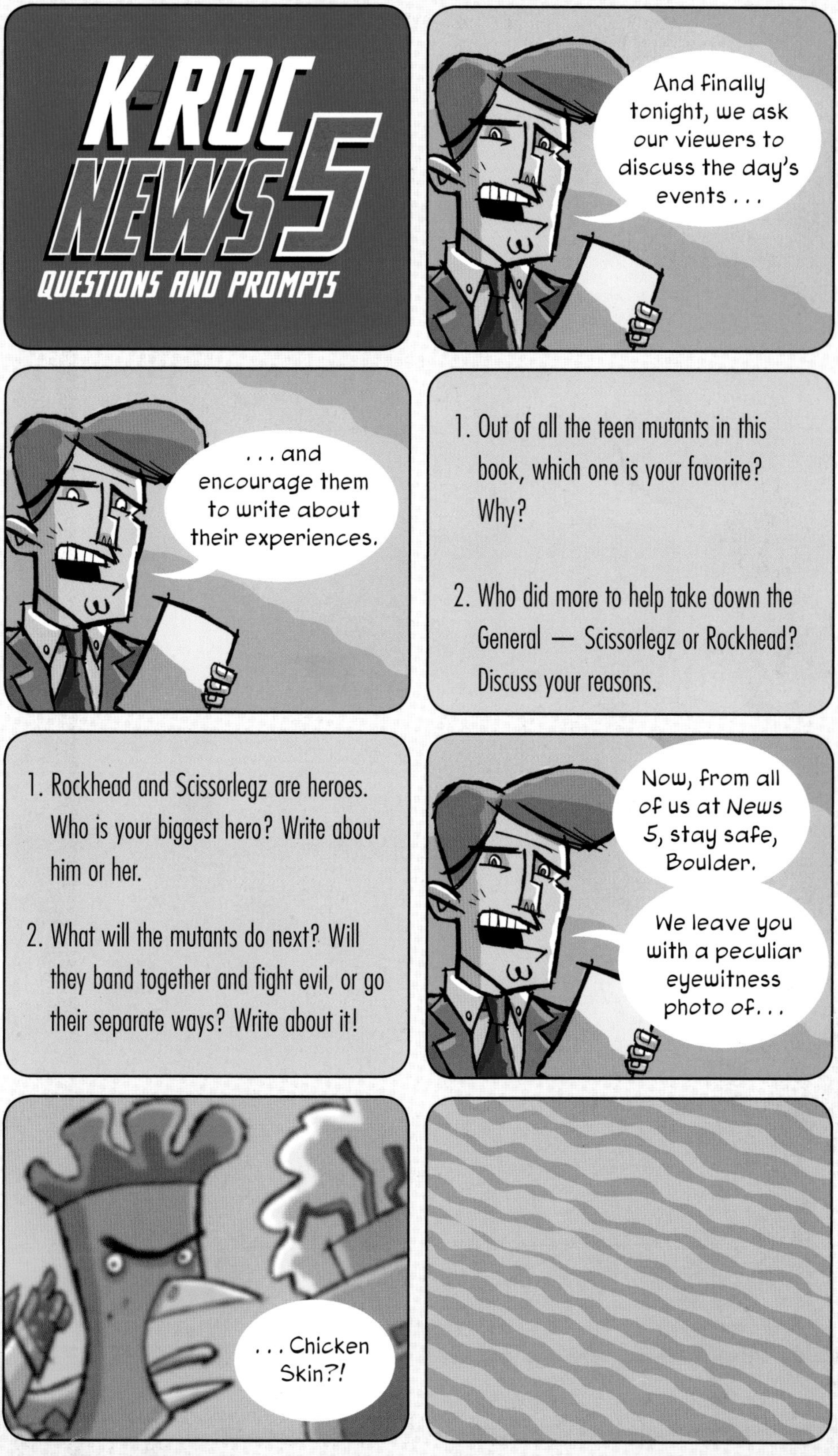
K-ROC NEWS 5
QUESTIONS AND PROMPTS
And finally tonight, we ask our viewers to discuss the day's events . . .
. . . and encourage them to write about their experiences.
1. Out of all the teen mutants in this book, which one is your favorite? Why?
2. Who did more to help take down the General — Scissorlegz or Rockhead? Discuss your reasons.
1. Rockhead and Scissorlegz are heroes. Who is your biggest hero? Write about him or her.
2. What will the mutants do next? Will they band together and fight evil, or go their separate ways? Write about it!
Now, from all of us at News 5, stay safe, Boulder.
We leave you with a peculiar eyewitness photo of. . .
. . . Chicken Skin?!

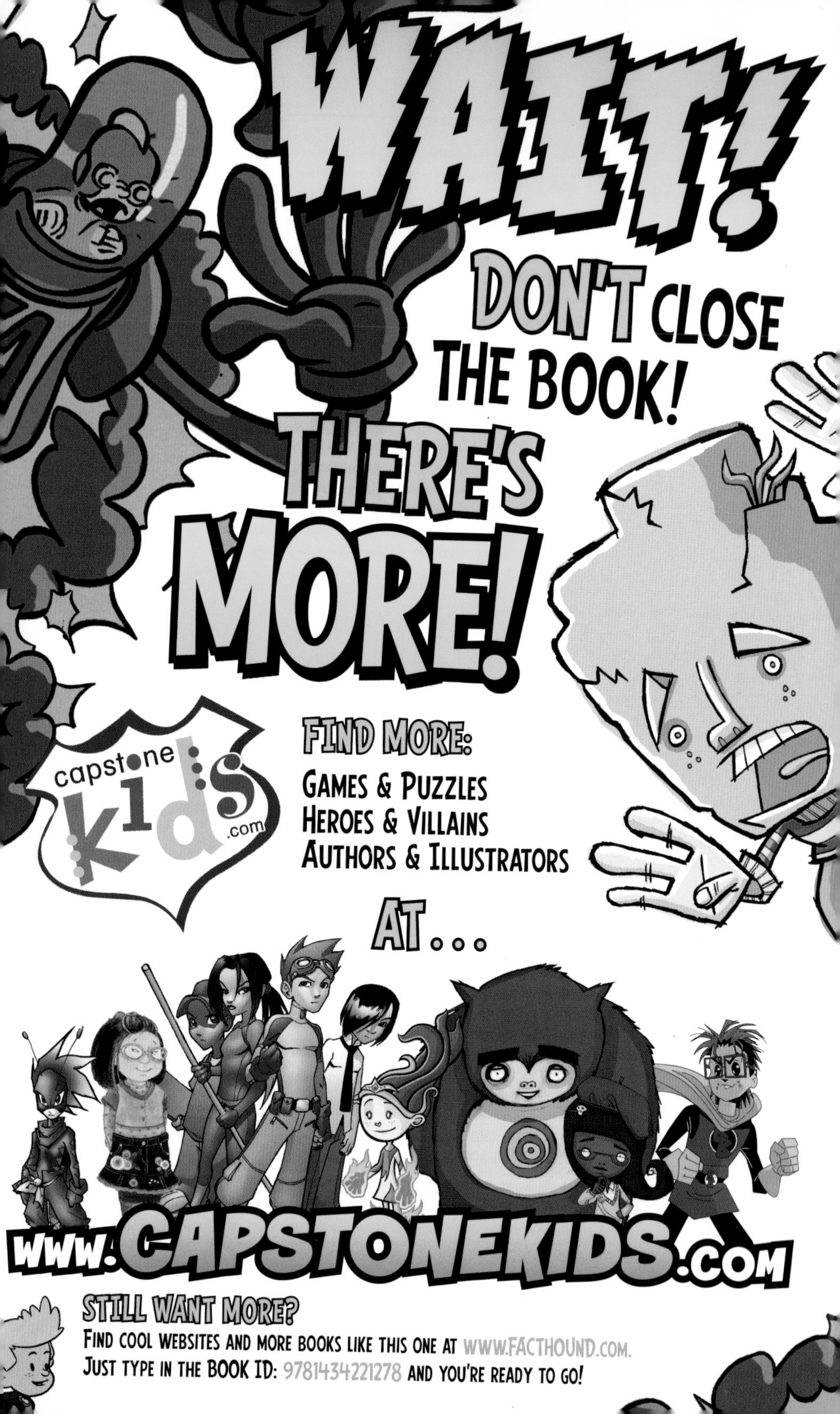
WAIT!
DON'T CLOSE THE BOOK!
THERE'S MORE!
FIND MORE:
GAMES & PUZZLES
HEROES & VILLAINS
AUTHORS & ILLUSTRATORS
AT...
capstone kids .com
WWW.CAPSTONEKIDS.COM
STILL WANT MORE?
FIND COOL WEBSITES AND MORE BOOKS LIKE THIS ONE AT WWW.FACTHOUND.COM.
JUST TYPE IN THE BOOK ID: 9781434221278 AND YOU'RE READY TO GO!